A Special Limited
Edition Hardback of

Steampunk Quartet 3:
THE LONDON
PARTICULAR

Signed by the Author

George Mann

This is copy: 38

THE LONDON PARTICULAR

NewCon Press Novellas

Set 1: Science Fiction (Cover art by Chris Moore)
The Iron Tactician – Alastair Reynolds
At the Speed of Light – Simon Morden
The Enclave – Anne Charnock
The Memoirist – Neil Williamson

Set 2: Dark Thrillers (Cover art by Vincent Sammy)
Sherlock Holmes: Case of the Bedevilled Poet – Simon Clark
Cottingley – Alison Littlewood
The Body in the Woods – Sarah Lotz
The Wind – Jay Caselberg

Set 3: The Martian Quartet (Cover art by Jim Burns)
The Martian Job – Jaine Fenn
Sherlock Holmes: The Martian Simulacra – Eric Brown
Phosphorous: A Winterstrike Story – Liz Williams
The Greatest Story Ever Told – Una McCormack

Set 4: Strange Tales (Cover art by Ben Baldwin)
Ghost Frequencies – Gary Gibson
The Lake Boy – Adam Roberts
Matryoshka – Ricardo Pinto
The Land of Somewhere Safe – Hal Duncan

Set 5: The Alien Among Us (Cover art by Peter Hollinghurst)
Nomads – Dave Hutchinson
Morpho – Philip Palmer
The Man Who Would be Kling – Adam Roberts
Macsen Against the Jugger – Simon Morden

Set 6: Blood and Blade (Cover art by Duncan Kay)
The Bone Shaker – Edward Cox
A Hazardous Engagement – Gaie Sebold
Serpent Rose – Kari Sperring
Chivalry – Gavin Smith

Set 7: Robot Dreams (Cover art by Fangorn)
According To Kovac – Andrew Bannister
Deep Learning – Ren Warom
Paper Hearts – Justina Robson
The Beasts Of Lake Oph – Tom Toner

THE LONDON PARTICULAR

A NEWBURY & HOBBES INVESTIGATION

George Mann

NEWCON
PRESS

NewCon Press
England

First published in the UK by NewCon Press
41 Wheatsheaf Road, Alconbury Weston, Cambs, PE28 4LF
September 2022

NCP289 (limited edition hardback)
NCP290 (softback)

10 9 8 7 6 5 4 3 2 1

ISBN:

978-1-914953-34-7 (hardback)
978-1-914953-35-4 (softback)

Cover art by Justin Tan
Back cover layout by Ian Whates

Editorial meddling by Ian Whates
Typesetting by Ian Whates

ONE

"Confounded things!"

Sir Charles Bainbridge, Chief Inspector of Scotland Yard, sagged back in his seat, glowering at his left shirt cuff in abject disgust. The small silver cufflink, crafted to resemble a tangled Celtic knot, dangled loose from the eyehole. "Flora always used to deal with the damned things for me," he muttered. "But whenever I try to do them..." He glanced out of the carriage window at the city lights, which were flitting by like a bright smear across the world.

Veronica saw Newbury stifle a grin.

"Here, Sir Charles – allow me," she said, leaning across to attend to the errant cuffs. Bainbridge had been mentioning his late wife more frequently in recent weeks, she'd observed, and she wondered if it was a symptom of how unsettled he was feeling, given the unfortunate developments with the Queen and her decision to wage war upon the fledgling Secret Service – an operation in which Bainbridge, unknown to Her Majesty, had become heavily embroiled. The three of them – Bainbridge, Newbury and herself – were, in essence, now engaged in a clandestine struggle against their own monarch. None of them were bearing the matter lightly. Even Newbury, despite his air of affected nonchalance.

Bainbridge inspected his cuff, and then nodded his thanks to Veronica. "I mean, what are we doing here, anyway?" he said. "The whole thing is a ruddy waste of time. Attending a damnable *party*, now, while the world falls to pieces around us? While a mad Queen orders the deaths of our friends and colleagues. Not to mention the spate of ugly murders currently plaguing the Yard, which should be commanding my attention. I can tell you this much, Newbury – I don't feel much in the mood for a celebration."

"You're hiding it remarkably well," said Newbury, with a sigh.

"And sarcasm is bound to help."

"Please try to cheer up, Charles. You know we have to keep up appearances. And if that means showing our faces at some silly society party to keep the Queen off our backs – well, needs must." Newbury shot Veronica a fleeting smile. "Besides, I'm looking forward to it. I'm told the desserts are quite excellent."

Bainbridge snorted. "Well, that's all right then. So long as there's a good *dessert*."

"There's a lot to be said for a well-timed dessert," said Newbury. "Good for the soul."

Bainbridge offered a non-committal grunt by way of reply and returned to studying his cuff.

Veronica sighed. She'd hoped the party was going to serve as a distraction from their daily woes. Heaven knew – they all needed it.

She eased back in her seat. Outside, the streets were wreathed in a diffuse, wispy fog that seemed to cling to the carriage as they hurtled down a narrow lane, before turning abruptly into the driveway of a large manor house.

"At last," said Newbury. "We're here."

The driver slowed the horses to a steady trot as they rumbled up the gravelled drive. Veronica couldn't discern much from where she was sitting, aside from a steady stream of black carriages and hansom cabs arriving ahead of them.

"It's busy," she said, as much for something to break the oppressive silence.

Newbury shrugged. "I'm not surprised. These parties have quite a reputation. People come from far and wide."

The carriage shuddered to a halt. The driver tapped lightly on the roof.

"Right then," said Veronica, getting to her feet. "Let's see what all the fuss is about." She opened the door and stepped out into the chill night air.

Newbury followed behind her.

"Thank you, driver," said Bainbridge, when he'd clambered down to join the others. "I shouldn't get too comfortable if I were you. I don't think we'll be staying long."

"Right you are, sir," replied the huddled man from up on the dickey box. "Just send for me when you want me."

"Good man." Bainbridge turned to regard Newbury and Veronica. "I suppose we should get this over and done with, then. And I promise – I'll make an effort to be as gregarious a guest as possible."

Newbury laughed, nudging his friend's arm playfully. "There's a first time for everything, eh?"

"Don't push it," muttered Bainbridge gruffly, his lips twitching in a smile he was unable to contain.

"Come on, let's go inside."

They started up the gravel path towards an impressive if somewhat unattractive manor house, here on the outskirts of Highgate. The architect had clearly favoured the gothic revivalist style of a few decades previous; the building was a cornucopia of turrets, arched windows, leering grotesques and high melodrama. Ivy rippled across the brickwork and a single gas lamp hung above the portico, fashioned in the style of a wrought iron candle sconce. It emitted a sickly yellow glow, deepening the shadows around the main entrance. Wispy fog was beginning to settle in murky puddles, stirring around their ankles as they traipsed up towards the door. Veronica could hear the chatter of raised voices spilling out from one of the rooms inside.

"It's... quite a venue," she said, drawing her shawl tighter around her shoulders.

"It's monstrous," said Bainbridge, keeping his voice low. At least, she considered, he had the good manners to keep his ill-tempered comments amongst friends.

"Our host, Greyson Fairfax, built the place about thirty years ago," said Newbury, "or so I'm led to believe. He inherited the land from his uncle, along with a crumbling old pile that hadn't seen much in the way of maintenance for a hundred years. The builders encouraged him to tear it down and start anew. Apparently there was little worth saving."

Bainbridge snorted, as if to say: *there's little worth saving now.* "You know this Fairfax chap?" he asked.

"By reputation," replied Newbury. "The man's a celebrated polymath: inventor, artist, architect, social reformer and confirmed bachelor."

"Good Lord," said Bainbridge. "Sounds as if the man's got some sort of messiah complex."

Newbury laughed. "Or perhaps he just likes to keep himself busy."

They continued trudging up the driveway towards the house, their footfalls stirring puddles of syrupy fog.

Ahead of them the door stood open, spilling light onto the mist-shrouded portico. It was thickening now, closing in around the building, stifling and tubercular, a true London particular. Veronica supposed she should have grown accustomed to such conditions long ago, but truth was she never failed to find it unsettling when the world was obscured behind such swirling, impenetrable murk, as if someone had draped a gauzy veil across the city. She was glad to be stepping inside for the evening. She followed Newbury in, Bainbridge bringing up the rear, his cane clacking loudly with every step.

Inside, far from echoing the gothic splendour of the exterior, the hallway was the picture of modernity, its walls painted a warm sage and decorated with stylised willow branches and water lilies. A thin, sweeping balustrade of brass traced the curve of a feature staircase, and multicoloured light filtered down through the stained-glass chandelier above, speckling the polished wooden floor in bright reds, blues and greens. Several doors led off into rooms on either side of the hallway – although most of them remained shut – and a passage disappeared down the left-hand side of the staircase, presumably towards the kitchens and the domain of the servants. An elderly valet in an impeccable black suit was standing just inside the doorway, and he peered at them expectantly, cocking his head slightly to one side in a curious gesture. His eyes looked glazed—he'd evidently had his fill of welcoming in his master's guests, and Veronica could hardly blame him; it was an onerous job, loitering in the draughty hallway, conjuring a smile for those who would hardly see him.

"Good evening," he said mechanically, the corner of his mouth twitching in the ghost of a smile, "and welcome to Fairfax House. You are?"

"Sir Maurice Newbury, Sir Charles Bainbridge and Miss Veronica Hobbes," said Newbury.

The valet nodded sagely, as if he had known the answer all along and were simply going through the motions and formalities. "Most welcome. All of you." Veronica rubbed her hands together to stave off the cold. Behind them, the fog was coiling around the open door inquisitively, reaching inside with tentative fingers. "Soames here will take your coats," continued the valet, gesturing behind him without looking. Another, smaller man with a fixed grin and dark, beady eyes stepped out from where he'd been loitering in the shadowy doorway of a side room. He was younger, too – around twenty – with dark hair and a pale complexion. He approached, trailing his left leg slightly in a limp. He held out his hands.

"If you please."

Veronica shrugged off her coat and scarf and handed them to the man. Newbury and Bainbridge did the same, piling up the bulky garments on the footman's outstretched forearms until the diminutive fellow was all but swamped beneath them.

"Can you manage?" asked Veronica.

"Soames will be fine," said the valet. The footman staggered away. Veronica watched as he disappeared into the side room. "Now, if you'd like to make your way through to the ballroom, pre-dinner drinks are being served. Most of the other guests have already arrived." He gestured to a set of double doors on the other side of the hallway.

"And Mr. Fairfax?" said Newbury. "I should very much like to thank our host for his kind invitation."

"Mr. Fairfax has just stepped away for a moment to see to a small matter," said the valet. "But he will no doubt return forthwith. I suggest you make yourselves at home and take a moment to mingle with the other guests while you wait." The valet cocked his head again in that same, odd affectation. "There is a considerably well stocked bar."

"A large brandy would certainly help to banish this interminable chill," muttered Bainbridge.

"And might go some way to lightening our mood," added Veronica. "Come along."

Newbury thanked the valet and followed quickly behind.

The double doors—folded back and propped open with weighty brass door stops in the form of horses' heads – opened onto an enormous chamber that might once have been the aforementioned ballroom but was now given over to housing an impressive array of Fairfax's mechanical inventions. Along one wall a bar had been set up, manned by a trio of impressive-looking automata that resembled nothing so much as human skeletons cast in brass, and plated with sheaths of the same, gleaming metal: armour against the hordes of thirsty guests clamouring for their attention. The automata's faces were blank plates slotted with a series of deep grooves, along which crude facsimiles of eyes, lips and brows travelled in straight lines, offering a degree of animation to what might otherwise have remained statuesque fixed expressions. All three of them were presently engaged in fulfilling orders, mechanically pouring and mixing an array of drinks.

On a pillar at the centre of the room – around which several more guests milled and chattered in small groups – the upper torso of another automaton had been mounted. This one was more of a bare skeleton, revealing the intricate clockwork mechanisms that articulated its joints, and its face was a smooth, polished plate, with no affectation or attempt to imitate human expression. It was presently engaged in playing – rather exquisitely – a familiar concerto for the violin, but Veronica, who had never been good at remembering the names of such things, could not easily place it.

Beside her, Newbury stood looking up at the thing with considerable glee. She tugged on his sleeve.

"Sorry," he said. "Were you saying something?"

"I wondered if you wanted a brandy."

Newbury grinned. "I'll fetch the drinks." He turned to glance at the bar. "I want to take a closer look at those remarkable machines."

Veronica laughed. "In that case, I'll have wine and soda. A large one."

"All right," said Newbury. "I'll be back in a moment." He set out for the bar, weaving his way through the knots of other guests. Veronica guessed there must have been twenty of them, at least, along with several members of serving staff, each of whom were wearing the same weary expression as the two men they'd met in the hallway. She eyed the other guests for a moment, looking for anyone she might know. The men were a sea of black and white evening suits, while the women were adorned with brightly coloured dresses and feather-crested hats. They had evidently all made an effort for the occasion. She was beginning to feel a little underdressed.

"Sir Charles! Is it really you?"

"I... um..."

"It *is* you! How wonderful."

Veronica turned to see Bainbridge, his eyes wide in sudden fear, had been cornered by a tall, slim woman in a blue dress. She was wearing a fur stole across her shoulders and a navy-blue hat was perched jauntily on her perfectly coiffed head. Her features were severe and immaculate, her cheeks tinged with a light hint of rouge, her lipstick a bold slash of red. Her gloved hand was resting on Bainbridge's forearm and the length of her hem was just a fraction short of decent. Veronica liked her immediately. Bainbridge, on the other hand, looked utterly terrified.

"It must be – what – three years since we saw you last? That beastly affair with the groundskeeper and those musty old remains in the gardens."

"I... well, yes, I suppose it is, Miss Fotheringhay. Three years. Yes."

The woman tutted. "Cynthia, please." She smiled wolfishly. "All my friends call me Cynthia, and we *are* friends, aren't we, Sir Charles?"

"What? Oh yes, of course."

"Excellent!" Her fingers tightened visibly around Bainbridge's wrist. Veronica saw him swallow. "Now, I think it's only right that I introduce you to my friend, Miss Margaret Welch. She's heard all about you, of course, and is positively dying to make your acquaintance." She made to drag him away, towards a small knot of women standing by the fireplace on the other side of the room."

"But... ah... Miss Hobbes," he stuttered, turning his head to shoot Veronica a pleading look.

Veronica stifled a laugh. "Oh, no. Don't mind me, Sir Charles. Please, make the most of the opportunity to catch up with your friend."

Miss Fotheringhay gave a beaming smile. "You see, Sir Charles? Miss Hobbes is more than happy to spare you for a short while. Come along, now."

Veronica was forced to bite her lip at the look of sheer horror on Bainbridge's face as he resigned himself to being led away. She watched for a moment as the small group of women fell upon him as if he were one of Newbury's much-lauded desserts.

Around her, the chatter of the party was in full swing. Newbury was still engaged at the drinks station, deep in conversation with another man while one of the automata measured out their drinks with meticulous, clockwork precision. She turned on the spot, drinking it all in. Perhaps Newbury was right – a party was exactly what they needed. An opportunity to forget themselves for an evening, to bury all the fear and worry and anxiety over the Queen, to stop being 'Miss Veronica Hobbes' and 'Sir Maurice Newbury' for a few hours; to just be themselves.

She watched a couple over by the window, caught in a sudden outburst of laughter, a shared joke, a fleeting moment of intimacy. The man put his hand on the woman's arm. And then the woman turned, as if sensing Veronica's eyes on her back, and all at once, Veronica was gasping, memories unscrolling at the sight of the familiar face: her old tutor, Juliet Clewes.

The woman still looked the same. A little careworn now, perhaps, with tighter lines around her small mouth and crow's feet by her eyes. But the smile was the same, generous and warm, and her eyes shone just as bright as they always had when they met Veronica's from across the room. Veronica hurried over, grinning broadly.

"Well, this is quite a surprise. How are you, Veronica?" The woman embraced her enthusiastically.

"Miss Clewes! It's so lovely to see you." Veronica glanced at the woman's companion. "Unless...?"

Miss Clewes laughed. "Oh, no. We're not *married*, dear. We prefer to keep things perfectly scandalous. Gives people something to talk about, doesn't it, Timothy?"

"Quite so, my dear," agreed the man, solemnly.

"*Miss Clewes!*"

"Oh, come now, dear. Call me Juliet. It's been years since you were in petticoats, and my tutoring days are long over."

"Very well. Juliet it is."

"Now, let me look at you." The woman held her at arm's length, looking her up and down appraisingly. "You've become quite the young lady, I see."

Veronica raised an eyebrow. "Less of the 'lady', thank you. I hold my own, just as you taught me."

"I'm glad to hear it." Miss Clewes beckoned her companion forward. "Timothy, this is Veronica Hobbes, a former protégé. One of my finest students, in fact."

"Oh, stop it," said Veronica.

"A pleasure," said the man, taking Veronica's hand and touching his lips to her fingers, like some gentleman from a Restoration play. There was a vague Scottish lilt to his words, although he hadn't yet spoken enough for Veronica to properly place it. It was clear that Miss Clewes was the one in the relationship with plenty to say – Veronica was pleased to see that she hadn't changed a bit.

"Timothy is a musician and composer," she added.

"How wonderful," said Veronica. She glanced at the automaton on the plinth behind her, the gentle strains of its

11

violin still washing over the crowd below, and then back at the man. He must have been ten years Miss Clewes's junior, with a pencil thin moustache and a full head of coarse black hair. He was smiling. "What do you make of all this?"

"By rights I should probably decry it as a travesty," he said, laughing, "make some argument that a machine will never be able to play with the emotion and fluidity of a human being…"

"But?"

"But truthfully I think it's all rather marvellous. Fairfax is evidently a genius."

"You've met him?"

Timothy shook his head. "Not yet. But I'm looking forward to it."

Juliet was looking over Veronica's shoulder. "I'm sure he was here when we arrived. That woman in the blue dress certainly seemed to think so."

Veronica was just about to tell her what the valet had said about Fairfax having to deal with some matter before dinner, when she saw Juliet's face break into a huge grin. Someone nudged her shoulder. She turned to see Newbury, clutching two large brandies and a glass of wine and soda. She took her drink. "Thanks."

"Well?" said Juliet.

Veronica offered her a confused look.

"Aren't you going to introduce us?"

"Oh, yes, sorry. This is Sir Maurice Newbury. My, umm…"

"Yes, dear?" The woman beamed. Her eyes seemed to twinkle.

"Oh, no," said Veronica, feeling her cheeks flush. "It's not like that. It's just… we're…"

"Friends," said Newbury. "We're dear friends."

Juliet cackled in delight. "Just like Timothy and I."

"Oh, no…"

"It's all right, dear. We're amongst friends."

"But –"

Juliet offered Newbury her hand. "Juliet Clewes," she said. "Veronica's former tutor."

"Ah," said Newbury. "How interesting."

"And this is my *friend*, Timothy Fraser."

The two men shook hands. "A pleasure," said Newbury. Veronica thought she might die of embarrassment.

"You're my kind of man, Sir Maurice," said Juliet.

"I am?"

"You're carrying two large brandies."

Newbury chuckled. "One's for Sir Charles, but he seems to have abandoned us."

"He's been accosted by a satisfied customer," said Veronica, nodding towards the fireplace.

Newbury smirked. "That'll work wonders for his mood."

"So – tell me about yourself, Veronica. What have you been doing since I saw you last?"

Veronica glanced at Newbury. He was clearly enjoying this. "Well, there's not really a lot to tell. I'm living in Kensington, and I work with Sir Maurice…"

"And what is it you do, Sir Maurice?" asked Timothy. He was fumbling nervously with his empty glass.

"Oh, a little bit of this and a little bit of that. I often help the police with their enquiries."

"How interesting. In what capacity?"

"I have a keen interest in humanity's foibles and belief systems. Folklore, mythology, ancient religions and the like. Sometimes I'm able to offer them a... different perspective."

"And you, too, Veronica?" asked Juliet.

Veronica nodded. "I do what I can to help."

"Well, I must say – the evening is certainly looking up. I expect to hear a lot more of your adventures over dinner." The woman opened her purse and extracted a thick, brown cigar, which she tapped against her chin as if in thought.

"Is that...?" ventured Veronica.

"Yes. I know. A filthy habit. But I do so enjoy it." Juliet grinned. "I'm not so inconsiderate as to offend the nostrils of others, however. Please, forgive me for a moment while I step outside." She started for the door.

"I'll replenish the drinks," said Timothy, making for the bar. "Miss Hobbes?"

"Oh, no. Thank you. But Juliet?" she said, calling after the other woman, who turned to look back over her shoulder. "Be careful, won't you? Only, the fog is settling out there. It'd be easy to lose your bearings."

Juliet gave a dismissive wave and carried on her way, plucking a canape from a serving platter as she went.

"She's quite a character," said Newbury.

"She certainly is." Veronica laughed. "It's been a long time."

"Stirring old memories?"

"Fond ones. I'd forgotten how free she is."

Newbury took a sip from his brandy. "It explains where you got it from."

"I suppose it does, rather."

Newbury nodded towards the fireplace, where Bainbridge was still fending off a clutch of adoring middle-aged women, who appeared to be encouraging him, rather strenuously, to entertain them with stories of his derring-do. He met Newbury's eyes from across the room, his expression pleading.

"Don't you think you should rescue him?" said Veronica.

"Not yet. I'm having too much fun watching him squirm."

Veronica laughed. "The poor man. They're eating him alive."

"It'll do him good. It's about time he tested the waters and opened himself up to the possibility of meeting someone new. A woman. He deserves it."

"There's testing the waters, and then thrashing about until you drown…"

Newbury laughed again. "You're not wrong. But look – here comes that valet again to call us in for dinner. Looks like Charles is saved after all."

The old valet – whose world-weary expression had barely altered since they'd encountered him in the hallway – stood beneath the arch of the double doors and jingled a small bell for attention. The hubbub of the gathered throng died away almost instantly, and the strains of the automaton's violin stilled.

"Dinner will be served momentarily in the dining room. Mr. Fairfax is pleased to request your presence." The valet gave a short bow from the waist, and then beckoned for people to begin filing through, back out into the hallway.

"Come on," said Newbury. "I'm famished." He drained the last of his brandy and placed the empty glass on a nearby side table. Then, with a shrug, he downed Bainbridge's too.

"What about Miss Clewes?"

"Perhaps we can save her a seat. I'm sure the staff will point her in the right direction when she's good and ready. She doesn't seem the type to be hurried."

Veronica gave a brief nod. "Yes, all right."

They followed the ambling crowd out into the hallway. Veronica felt the chill from the open door as a cold breath upon the nape of her neck, and she glanced in that direction, hoping to catch a glimpse of Juliet loitering in the doorway. There was no sign. An impenetrable cloak of fog had descended outside the house, thick and grey, rippling into the building like waves lapping at a shoreline, swirling now around the foot of the stairs.

"Don't you think you should close the door now that everyone's here?" she heard a man say to the valet. "Before that pea-souper swallows all of us up, what?"

"Oh, yes, sir," the valet muttered. "I'll see to it just as soon as everyone is seated."

They shuffled through into the dining hall, where a huge mahogany table dominated the centre of the long chamber. Places had been set around its entire circumference, including a gilded, throne-like chair at its head – evidently intended for their mysterious host. A crackling fire roared in the immense stone fireplace, and gloomy portraits looked down with austere, disapproving expressions from the walls. A row of tall windows that would have looked out upon the extensive gardens revealed only the swirling miasma beyond. The thing that caught Veronica's attention, however, was the delightful, mechanised centrepiece that rose from a depression in the heart of the table. It was around four foot high and six foot long and whirred and clacked with an impressive array of moving parts, describing, in miniature, a series of scenes from a circus, from tiny trapeze artists to knife throwers, lion tamers to dancing elephants. It was a thing of wonder, like the brass workings of a clock writ large, and the other guests were already crowding around the table to watch the little show cycle through its joyous performance.

"Would you look at that," said Newbury. "The sheer workmanship..." He crossed to the table, resting both palms upon the surface as he leaned closer, admiring the wondrous machine.

"You do realise we've lost him for the rest of the evening now, don't you?"

Veronica turned to see that Bainbridge had finally managed to extricate himself from the gaggle of women and was standing just behind her, a generous glass of brandy in his hand. "I'm glad to see the same can't be said for you, Sir Charles."

Bainbridge grimaced. "It was a close-run thing, I assure you." He glanced sheepishly at the woman in the blue dress, then winced when he saw her give a little wave. He took a long draw from his glass. Veronica had to give Newbury credit, though – despite his protestations to the contrary, Bainbridge's mood had clearly improved. "So, any sign of our absent host?"

"Not as yet," said Veronica. "Although I'm half expecting some sort of grand entrance at any moment."

"Mmmm," muttered Bainbridge. "It does seem he has a flair for the theatrical. Which goes some way to explaining why Newbury is so taken with him."

Around the table people were beginning to take their seats. Veronica looped her arm through Bainbridge's and led him over. "Come along, before you're accosted again."

"Heaven forbid."

They shuffled Newbury around the edge of the table until they found several unoccupied seats. "Here, Sir Maurice – if you could place my bag on that seat unt-"

An ear-splitting shriek cut through the chatter.

It had come from outside – Veronica knew it immediately. The sound of a woman, terrified for her life; the ragged, raw, primal scream of fear.

"Juliet."

She didn't wait to see what the others were doing; how the other guests had responded to the call. She thrust her chair back and launched herself towards the door. Newbury barked her name and hurried after her. She vaguely heard Bainbridge bellowing at the room for calm.

Out in the hallway, Timothy Fraser was already running for the front door, while the valet stood gaping, his mouth slack-jawed in apparent shock.

"Timothy, wait!" she gasped as she lurched across the hallway, where visibility had been compromised by the cloying fog that was still curling in from outside. He stopped, framed in the doorway for a moment as he glanced back at her, a look of sheer terror on his face, and then turned and plunged into the miasma, bellowing Juliet's name.

Veronica felt a hand on her arm. "Wait, Veronica. Please." She allowed Newbury to pull her to a stop, just before the open door. Outside, she could see nothing of the driveway or the portico through which they'd entered. It was as if the house had been set adrift, excised neatly from its anchor in the real world, and now floated somewhere amongst dream-like clouds. Only these clouds promised to seep into one's lungs, to embrace you as fully as they'd embraced the house.

"We need to stick together," said Newbury. "If we go too far, we might not be able to find our way back in this."

"But Juliet... You heard that scream as well as I did."

"We'll find her, Veronica. But we'll do it together."

She nodded and held out her hand. He clasped it tight, and together they ran out into the mist-choked night.

From the doorway of the dining room, Bainbridge watched them racing off. A part of him thought he should go after them, but he fought the urge. Newbury was right – it would be too easy to get lost out there, and he risked becoming just another missing person they'd have to find. As things stood, it was looking as though Fairfax was going to have to find a way to put them all up until the morning; people could not be expected to set out for home in such dangerous conditions.

Speaking of which – where was the man? Theatrics or not, it was high time the man showed himself, to reassure his guests.

Bainbridge turned his attention back to the dining hall, where the other guests had all returned to their seats. They were looking at him expectantly. He sighed. "For those who may not know me, my name is Sir Charles Bainbridge, of Scotland Yard. Please, rest assured, my associates Sir Maurice and Miss Hobbes will get to the bottom of whatever has happened outside. No doubt there's been an accident, due in part to the impaired visibility. I'd advise you all to remain inside – the conditions have worsened to the point where it is impossible to navigate the fog. I shall be speaking to our host to discuss the necessary arrangements for us to sit things out here until it is safe." He peered at the sea of blank faces. "Has anyone seen Mr. Fairfax yet this evening?"

There was a murmur from amongst the other guests, along with a series of shrugs and headshakes.

"Then I suggest you all remain seated while I go and seek him out."

Pinching the bridge of his nose to stave off what felt like the onset of a headache, he turned and left the room.

She could hardly breathe for the thick, swirling miasma. It pressed against her skin, clammy and cold, shedding droplets of moisture in her hair, on her clothes, her lips. She gripped Newbury's hand tighter, turning on the spot, searching for any break in the pallid grey, any sign that she was still tethered in the real world. She felt as if she'd been suddenly cut loose, the moment she'd stepped through the door. It was like a wall enclosing her from every direction. She could no longer see the house, or even the faint glow of the lights from the windows. The world had shrunk to just her and Newbury and the tiny patch of gravel upon which they stood.

"Juliet?" called Newbury, his left hand cupped around his mouth. "Timothy?"

Even the sound of his voice seemed deadened by the foggy shroud.

There was no reply.

Veronica took a step forward. She narrowed her eyes. A dark shape loomed out of the grey; a hulking shadow, towering above her head. She tugged lightly on Newbury's hand. "There's something here."

He turned, stepping forward, his arm stretched out before him as if to ward off any danger. They edged closer. The shape resolved.

"It's a carriage," said Newbury.

Veronica could see it now, the curve of the wheels, the sweep of the roof. One of the carriages they'd seen parked on the driveway as they'd come up to the house. How long had it been? No more than an hour, surely, but the world had changed utterly in that short time. And still there was no sign of Juliet. The woman had only stepped out to smoke a cigar.

"Juliet?"

"Timothy?"

A crunch of gravel from somewhere off to her right. She turned towards the sound but could see nothing. "Juliet?" she called again.

A sound like grinding gears. The hiss of something pneumatic.

"Did you hear that?" she hissed to Newbury.

"I did. And whatever it is, it's getting closer." He slipped his hand from hers, flexing his shoulders, rolling his neck.

And then another noise from somewhere behind them: the sickening sound of breaking bones, and a man's pained and terrified whimper.

"Now listen here, I demand that you tell me, right now: where is the master of this house?"

The valet cocked his head to the side in that same, curious gesture Bainbridge had noticed earlier, and smiled. "The master is currently indisposed. I'm certain he'll be with you all soon. If you'd like to return to your seat, dinner will be served shortly."

Bainbridge felt his cheeks flush. "I will *not* return to my seat! Something's not right here. Who invites twenty people over for dinner and then doesn't show up?"

"The master is currently —"

"Indisposed, yes. I heard you the first time. But frankly, that's not good enough. Doesn't he care that his guests are concerned? That arrangements need to be made in the face of this damnable fog? That someone's probably hurt themselves out there on his premises, and my friends are currently doing their best to find them before they die of ruddy exposure?" Bainbridge could barely contain himself. "One might imagine that you, sir, as valet to Mr. Fairfax, might deign to show a little more concern yourself!"

The valet simply offered that same inane smile. "I'm sure it won't be long now, sir. The master will be with us again soon."

"For God's sake," muttered Bainbridge. "Then I'll find him myself."

He turned his back on the infuriating man and stormed down the passageway that led alongside the staircase, intent on opening the door to every room until he found Mr. Greyson Fairfax and gave the man a piece of his mind.

"Timothy! Timothy, are you there? Can you hear me?"

Veronica charged through the fog towards the origin of the horrible sound. The whimpering had stopped now, but the strange mechanical footsteps persisted, trudging in her wake at a slow and sinister pace. Newbury was at her side, his breathing short and ragged.

"It's no use," he said. "We'll never find him in this."

"Timothy?" she called. "Juliet?"

The silence that followed was as terrifying as the screams that had preceded it.

"We can't give up now," she said, slowing her pace. "He's got to be around here some..." She trailed off as her eyes scanned the ground before her.

A man's foot, there on the gravel, black shoe gleaming with shiny polish. The rest of the leg, above the calf, disappeared into the fog. She recognised the trouser fabric immediately – the suit Timothy Fraser had been wearing.

"Here!" she said, beckoning Newbury over. "He must have fallen. Help me."

They hurried over.

"Timothy? Timo-" She stopped abruptly, her hand involuntarily covering her mouth.

The leg ended just above the knee. Thick, glossy blood pooled on the driveway, oozing from the ragged stump. "Oh no. *No.*"

She felt Newbury's hand on her back. "I'm so sorry," he murmured, before dropping to his haunches to examine the errant limb. Carefully, he picked it up, examining the wound around the stump. Veronica thought she might be sick.

"Whatever did this to him is immensely powerful. The limb has literally been torn in two. The femur has been snapped clean through."

"And... what about the rest of him?" said Veronica. "Perhaps he got away, passed out from the pain..."

Newbury simply shook his head. "I'm sorry. The blood loss alone..."

"But... what could have done such a thing?"

The ponderous footsteps sounded from the murk behind them.

"I very much fear we're about to find out..."

Bainbridge tried another door.

This time it opened readily, swinging aside on well-oiled hinges. He peered inside. A single gas lamp cast a warm, amber glow – a tiny sun, throwing much of the room into shadow. The room was evidently a library, lined with dark, towering bookcases, serried ranks of leatherbound spines bulging from every shelf. It reminded him of Newbury's drawing room, only considerably tidier. A single window had been covered by a heavy velvet drape, and aside from a large, free standing globe – that appeared to date from a long-forgotten era – the only other furniture in the room was a heavy mahogany desk and chair at the far end of the room. The scent of stale tobacco hung heavy in the air, along with a faint metallic tang.

Bainbridge knew immediately that something was wrong.

He could see a man was on his hands and knees behind the desk, his rear end jutting rudely into the air, as if he were scrabbling about on the floor after for some object he'd dropped.

Bainbridge entered the room, clearing his throat. "Mr. Fairfax?"

The man didn't reply.

Bainbridge's sense of unease increased exponentially. "Mr. Fairfax, I'm sorry to intrude, but I really must speak with you as a matter of some urgency."

When the man didn't move or even acknowledge his presence, Bainbridge crossed the room, the tip of his cane clicking against the marble floor.

"Mr. Fairfax? Is that you?"

He stood before the desk. Still the man didn't move.

"Come along, man! Your guests need you."

He rounded the desk, already anticipating the worst.

The man was dead, his neck twisted at an unnatural angle, one of his arms viciously removed from its socket. Blood had soaked into the long pile of the rug beneath him, staining the ragged edge of his white shirt a deep crimson. His eyes – milky and already beginning to putrefy – stared up at Bainbridge in abject horror from a taut face. The mouth was open, tongue stiff and swollen. His hair, once neatly oiled and swept back from his forehead, was now mussed and awry. He was clean shaven, although beads of spattered blood had dried on his pale cheeks.

"God damn it," muttered Bainbridge. "God damn it all."

He stood over the corpse for a moment, letting the sight of it permeate his thoughts, seeking any clues, any indication of what had happened to the man, how he had come to be face down on the floor behind a desk in the library. Was this even Fairfax? He'd need to find someone who could identify their errant host.

"You shouldn't be in here," said a voice from the other end of the room. He looked up to see the valet, watching him from the open doorway with dark, impassive eyes. The man stepped inside, pulling the door shut behind him. "You should have stayed in the dining room with the others." The valet took a step forward, cocking his head to one side. "Now what are we going to do, hmm?"

TWO

Veronica tensed.

She could see the shape of the thing now, looming out of the swirling fog, a silhouette against the stark grey night. It had the form of a human being but was taller – at least seven foot – with long, gangly arms and powerful, trunk-like legs. The whirring of gears and the chiming of clockwork accompanied each movement, along with the systematic hiss of escaping steam.

It raised its arm, claw-like fingers reaching for her…

"Come on!" she bellowed, grabbing for Newbury's sleeve. She tugged him to his feet from where he'd been crouching over Timothy's remains, backing them away from the oncoming terror.

"Wait…" he said, holding her back. "I want to see it. I need to understand what we're up against."

The *thing* – clearly some sort of monstrous machine – took another step forward, its glittering brass fingers puncturing the fog as they reached for Newbury, only inches away from his face. They were caked in dark, congealed blood.

"Newbury…"

"Almost… almost…"

Another step forward, and the automaton's head swam into view, parting the wall of grey as if pushing its way through the veil between worlds; as if being born from some surreal unreality, made corporeal before their very eyes. It bore a long, tapered beak where a man's mouth and nose would have been, and above that, two shining glass eyes that swivelled on twin axes like tiny mirrors, catching what faint light had managed to penetrate the vaporous blanket. The dome of its head was smooth brass, engraved or inlaid with elaborate filigree.

"All right," said Newbury, taking a step back, still facing the deadly automaton. His fingers scrabbled blindly for Veronica's, and then found them, interlacing and squeezing tight. "On my mark..." She held her breath. "*Now!* Run!"

Together they turned and fled into the gloom.

"Now look here!" said Bainbridge, striding determinedly towards the valet. His fingers tightened around the head of his cane. "I don't know what you think is going on here, but it seems to me you've got some explaining to do."

The valet cocked his head in that same, infuriating manner. "I do?"

"For god's sake, man! Your master is lying dead on the floor over there, and you're carrying on as if nothing's the matter! What's wrong with you?"

The valet raised his hand, gently pushing Bainbridge to one side as he strode past. He crossed to the desk, where he stood over the body for a moment, before slowly shaking his head. He seemed not in the least bit disturbed by the grisly sight of the corpse. "This is not my master," he said coolly, as if that was an end to the matter.

How could the man seem so unmoved?

"It's not?" asked Bainbridge. "You mean to tell me that man is *not* Greyson Fairfax?"

The valet looked at him, his expression blank. "Yes," he stated simply, before turning back to regard the body again.

"Then who the Devil is it, and what is he doing here?"

The valet seemed to consider this for a moment. "It is most unfortunate," he said. "Most unfortunate indeed. He is one of the guests. Mr. Edwin Blythe."

Bainbridge rubbed at his temple. That headache wasn't going anywhere fast. There was something peculiar going on here. He knew valets were schooled in dealing with the unexpected but this went beyond the pale. "I'd say it was a little more than unfortunate, man! One of your master's guests is *dead*. Bloody well torn apart, too, from what I can see. Which can only mean one thing."

"It can?"

"Yes! Someone in this house is a killer." Bainbridge took a deep breath and let it out. He couldn't allow his frustration with the valet to cloud his thinking. "Unless they've already made a break for it in this interminable fog, of course." It was the perfect cover for a clean getaway. He wondered how Newbury and Veronica were getting on out there. Could the killer have struck down Blythe in the library, before fleeing into the fog and encountering the Clewes woman as he made his escape? It was possible. "Where is Fairfax now?"

"As I have already explained," said the valet, his voice level, "he is presently indisposed."

"Well, he'd better get himself ruddy disposed, and quickly," snapped Bainbridge. "Is *he* responsible for this? It'll do you no good trying to cover for him. You'd be better spitting it out now. Is this why Fairfax hasn't shown his face this evening?"

"No. Under no circumstances could the master be involved in this man's death. I am certain of it."

"Well, we'll see about that. Now go. Go and fetch him. This is a matter for the police now, and I shall entertain no excuses." He was going to have to deal with this himself. There was no way the Yard would be able to get anyone else over to the house until the fog had lifted, and he had the other guests to consider. One of them could be responsible. Equally, more of them could be at risk. Without even an idea of what had transpired here, or any sense of motive, he had to assume the worst. Thank God that Newbury and Veronica were here to help him.

The valet gave a curt nod. "I shall convey your message to the master now."

"You do that," said Bainbridge, stepping to one side to let the valet pass.

He waited until the man had disappeared into the hallway, before crossing back to the desk to stand over the body, trying to discern anything he could that might help him to understand what had happened.

"Well, Mr. Edwin Blythe," he muttered. "So much for my night off."

"Which way?"

"I don't know. I think it must be that way."

The ponderous mechanical tread sounded closer again, and neither of them knew which way to turn. No light, no sound beside those terrible footfalls, seemed to penetrate the gloom. Veronica felt utterly disorientated. For all she knew, they'd been running in circles out here for the last few minutes.

"Come on," said Newbury, pulling her to the left. Behind them, the monstrous automaton altered direction in pursuit.

"How does it know which way to go?" she said, between ragged gasps.

"It must be tracking us by sound," replied Newbury. He was stumbling forward into the mist, waving his outstretched arm before him. He stopped suddenly, turning to glance back at her. "Here."

"What?"

"It's another parked carriage." She stepped closer, and the shape of the vehicle resolve before her. "That means the house should be directly behind us," she reasoned.

Newbury nodded. Before he could reply, the side of the carriage exploded. Veronica winced as airborne splinters stung the flesh of her cheeks and forearms; she saw streaks of bright blood bloom on Newbury's exposed face, and then a claw-like hand reached through the carriage wall, opening and closing spasmodically as it tried to grasp Newbury from behind. All the while, the steady, trudging footsteps continued towards them.

"There's two of them!"

"At least," said Newbury, edging away from the ruined carriage. "We've got to get back to the house. You make a run for it and I'll try to hold them off."

"Don't be ridiculous. We go together, as we always do." She gripped his hand, dragging him away. "It can't be that far."

They hurtled blindly through the greyness in the direction of the house, the two automata falling in behind them.

This time, they were not disappointed. The glow from the ballroom window dawned from the murk like a rising sun, and they hurried towards it before skidding to the right, skirting the side of the house as they made for the front door.

Veronica could hear the automata steadily gaining on them but dared not look back. Her heart was in her mouth. How had this happened? What had started out as a party had turned into a bloody massacre. Poor Juliet…

And then they were at the still-open door, tumbling through into the mist-shrouded hallway and almost going heel over head. Newbury righted himself, lurching for the heavy wooden door. With a groan of effort, he slammed it shut and hurriedly turned the key in the lock.

He fell back, gasping for breath, as a series of dull thuds sounded on the other side of the oak panels. He glanced at Veronica, clearly wondering whether the door would hold – they'd both seen what it had done to the carriage – but then the automata seemed to suddenly give up. The banging ceased, and after a moment, the sound of their footsteps receded into the night as they slowly trudged away.

"Newbury?" Veronica turned to see Bainbridge standing by the foot of the stairs, a grim expression on his face. "It seems we have a problem."

"You're right, Charles."

"I am?"

"Yes. We do have a problem." Newbury stood from where he'd been crouched examining the body of Edwin Smythe. He smoothed the front of his jacket. "He's been dead since yesterday."

"*Yesterday?*"

"Or at least the early hours of this morning. You can tell by the temperature and the way the blood has settled, not to mention the rigidity of the –"

"Yes, yes, Newbury. Spare us the details." Bainbridge chewed the edge of his moustache. "But it makes no sense. That valet said he was one of the party guests."

31

"But why lie? Unless he has something to hide." Newbury glanced toward the door. "Where is he? I didn't see him when we came back in."

"I sent him off to find Fairfax," said Bainbridge, "but he's taking his bloody time."

"He does seem to be dressed for a party," said Veronica. She was standing by the bookcase on the other side of the desk, listening to the two men with interest.

"I'm sorry?" said Bainbridge, glancing up.

"Mr. Smythe. Look at him. He's wearing a dinner jacket and tie. And it looks rather fine, too."

"You're right," said Newbury. "So, Blythe, whoever he is, wasn't here to see Fairfax over business. It wasn't even a social call."

"You're saying he *was* a party guest?" said Bainbridge.

"Perhaps," said Newbury. "But not at *tonight's* party."

Veronica frowned. "You think Fairfax had another party here last night?"

Newbury shrugged. "It's all supposition at this stage. All we know is that we've got a dead man, dressed in finery, who's been lying on the floor of this library for about a day."

Bainbridge grunted. "Do you think it could have been one of those machines you met outside? You said they'd... um... dismembered that man, Timothy." He glanced apologetically at Veronica.

They'd hurriedly filled Bainbridge in about the things out there, stalking them in the fog, and Newbury's supposition that they might have been an invention of Fairfax's that had somehow gone awry – perhaps originally intended as 'guard dogs' or some other form of security. It wouldn't have been the first time they'd encountered such things, after all – whenever people had tried to give machines a semblance of life, in Veronica's experience, it was destined to go horribly wrong.

"It would seem the most logical explanation," said Newbury, "although from what limited experience I have of them, it doesn't seem to fit their *modus operandi*."

"What are you talking about? He's had his arm ripped off, hasn't he?"

"Yes. But why dump him behind the desk in here? An area that's supposed to be off limits to party guests. It's as if they were hiding him. They didn't seem so concerned about that a few minutes ago," said Newbury.

"Perhaps their malfunction is getting worse," ventured Veronica. "Or they're using the smog as cover."

"Perhaps," echoed Newbury, in a way that told her that he remained unconvinced. "The key to all of this is Fairfax. If he can answer some of our questions we might be able to make sense of all this."

"If we can ever lay eyes on the fellow," spat Bainbridge. "You'd think he'd have the decency to show his face, if not for his guests then after several people have been killed on his premises."

"What about the other guests?" asked Veronica. They'd come straight to the library after meeting Bainbridge in the hallway. She had no sense of how much the other partygoers had been told.

"Oh, they're all merrily getting on with their dinner," said Bainbridge. "I thought it best to let them carry on for the meanwhile. We don't want to stir up any panic."

Newbury nodded. "Be that as it may, they need to know. We can't have any of them going wandering about the house or grounds. And none of us are getting out of here tonight. Not until the fog clears and we can deal with those damn sentries."

"At least we know none of them are responsible for Edwin Smythe," said Bainbridge, "assuming your assertions are correct about the time of death."

"I'm no pathologist, Charles, but I'm right about this."

Bainbridge nodded. "So that leaves Fairfax, if it wasn't one of his machines running riot."

"Or the staff," added Veronica.

"Or the staff," agreed Bainbridge. "There's definitely something untoward about that valet, for a start."

"Then we'll put him and the other staff to the question, too," said Newbury. "But first – how do you want to handle the guests?"

Bainbridge sighed. "I suppose you'd better leave that to me."

A hush fell over the seated diners as Newbury, Bainbridge and Veronica entered the room. It was clear from the state of the dinner plates, the array of empty bottles and the flush of people's cheeks, that the meal had continued in their absence. All sense of concern amongst the guests seemed to have dissolved, replaced by the warm glow of alcohol and comfort. It was as if they'd all forgotten the drama of earlier, and the horrible sound of Juliet's scream.

Veronica tried not to judge them too harshly – but it was an uphill struggle.

Several waiters were loading up a wooden trolley with the debris of the meal. Veronica felt her stomach growl, despite herself. She hadn't eaten for hours.

"Sir Charles!" called Miss Fotheringhay, raising her hand to give him a wave from across the other side of the room. "What news? I trust you and your friends have unravelled our little mystery? We've been taking wagers while you were gone."

Veronica grimaced. *Wagers?*

Bainbridge cleared his throat. "Now, I'd like everyone to stay calm and remain in your seats. I have some unfortunate news to share with you."

"It's Fairfax," whispered one of the other guests – a willowy looking woman in a pale dress – to her hirsute companion. "He's probably got a fever or something and is calling the whole night off."

"There's been a murder," said Bainbridge, cutting the woman to the quick. "Several murders, in fact." He paused to allow the news to sink in. There was a collective intake of breath. Even the waiters had stopped to listen, although their expressions gave nothing away.

"Is that... Was that...? What I mean to say is... that *scream?*" stammered an Indian man with neatly clipped hair and a long, tapered beard. He drummed his fingertips nervously on the table top, his eyes searching Bainbridge's face for a response.

"Yes," confirmed Newbury, from beside Bainbridge. "Unfortunately, the man who went to her aid was also killed by the same hand."

A murmur rippled around the table.

"Who?" said an imperious-looking man with a shock of white hair. "Whose hand?"

Veronica stepped forward. "There are machines out there in the fog. Automata. Whether they were built for this purpose, or whether they are malfunctioning, we can only guess. There are at least two of them, maybe more, and their entire purpose seems to be…" She faltered for a moment, before taking a deep breath, "seems to be to capture and dismember anyone who steps outside."

"*Dismember!*"

"Oh, God!"

"Heaven help us!"

"What's the meaning of this? Where's Fairfax?"

"Who's that woman they killed?"

Bainbridge allowed the panic to rumble on for a moment, before puffing out his chest and slamming the heel of his cane on the ground three times in quick succession. "You will be *quiet!*" he bellowed, glancing from one guest to the other as they slowly returned to their seats, cowed by this sudden demonstration of authority.

He waited for a moment longer, just to make his point. "What is more, there is a third body. A man by the name of Edwin Smythe, who may or may not have been a guest of Mr. Fairfax here last night. This time, the body was found in the library, also partially dismembered. So far, we have been unable to locate Mr. Fairfax for comment." Someone began to speak, and Bainbridge raised his hand, cutting them off. "This, I shall now take upon myself to rectify. Our missing host has a great many questions to answer. In the meantime, I ask that you all remain here, together, in this room. Under no circumstances are you to venture outside, and I encourage you not to wander the halls of the house." He paused. "That goes for you, too," he then added, indicating the three waiters. "I shall want to talk to you later."

"What if one needs to make use of the facilities?" said a wide-eyed woman, who appeared to be accompanying the white-haired man who'd spoken earlier.

"Then I suggest you cross your legs," said Bainbridge, brusquely. Then, with a sigh: "Or at the very least, travel in groups of no less than three, with only one group to leave this room at a time."

"This is ridiculous!" growled the white-haired man. "You cannot keep us prisoners here against our will."

"No," said Bainbridge. "I can't. You must feel free to go and get yourselves killed at any point." He turned his back on the room to face Newbury and Veronica. Behind him, everyone started talking at once.

"Right. That's that done."

"Quite," said Newbury. "Although I can't see them sitting on their hands for long, can you?"

"No," agreed Veronica. "They're scared and restless."

"And pompous with it," muttered Bainbridge. "I'd suggest the two of you remain here to keep an eye on things. I'm going to chase down that valet and find out what the Devil has happened to Fairfax."

"Sir Charles, you can't go wandering about on your own. You've just said yourself —"

"Miss Hobbes, I assure you, it's a necessity. And besides, I'm armed." He hefted his cane to underline his point.

"Be that as it may, if there are more of those automata wandering the halls…"

"… I shall hurry in the opposite direction." He smiled. "I'll be back shortly, with Fairfax and that valet in tow. You try to stop this lot from getting any bright ideas of their own."

"Easier said than done," said Newbury. "Be careful, Charles."

Bainbridge nodded and took a step towards the door.

"Sir Charles! Please, wait a moment." Bainbridge stopped, then turned to see who had spoken. It was the bearded Indian man who'd asked a question earlier. He crossed to join Bainbridge.

"What is it?" said Bainbridge.

"My name is Singh. Arun Singh. I'm an old friend of Greyson's. Fairfax, I mean. Greyson Fairfax."

"Yes?"

"Well, I thought perhaps I could be of some assistance. I know the house, you see. And I know Greyson. I can help you find him."

Bainbridge frowned, as if he was about to refuse the man, but then appeared to have a change of heart. "Yes, yes. All right. Thank you. Where do you propose we start?"

"Upstairs. His workshops. He's probably got caught up with some new invention and lost track of the time."

"Very good. Lead on then, Mr. Singh. Lead on."

An hour passed as if time itself had become mired in molasses. Several of the guests had pulled their chairs round into a semi-circle before the fireplace and were lounging there, twittering away with their vacuous conversation and gossip – no doubt an effort to keep occupied and hold any darker thoughts at bay.

Others were coping less well with the terms of their temporary lockdown.

"Who does he think he is, keeping us locked up in here like this? Doesn't he know I fought the Boers, hmmm?"

"I'm scared, Ted. I wish you could take me home."

"I'll give it another half hour, but if there's no news by then, I'm out of here, whether there's supposed monsters in the fog or not."

"Well, *I've* not seen anything."

Veronica sighed and glanced over at Newbury, who was perched on the edge of a dining chair, staring pensively at the door. He must have felt her eyes upon him, as he turned to meet her gaze, offering her the fleeting wisp of a smile. It was gone before she could even respond in kind, replaced by a dark, brooding aspect. She knew he'd rather be out there, with Bainbridge, *doing* something. She felt the same. But Bainbridge had been right – someone needed to keep an eye on the other guests, so they didn't go getting themselves killed. She only wished Bainbridge would hurry up. The tension in the room was palpable, and she knew that before long, people's patience was going to run out. She could hardly blame them.

She peered out of the window, hopeful that the ever-present fog might have finally started to recede, but it was not to be – the gloomy veil was as opaque as ever.

Veronica looked up at the sound of people moving about. It was the man with the white hair and his wife, both of whom had been particularly vocal during Bainbridge's briefing earlier. They made a beeline for the door.

"Where do you think you're going?" said Newbury, seemingly unfurling as he rose from where he'd been sitting.

"Home," said the man. He stared at Newbury confrontationally. "We've had just about as much of this ridiculous situation as we can take."

Newbury shrugged, then sat back down on the edge of his chair. "Well, you've been warned, sir. I cannot make things any clearer for you. Go outside, and you will both likely die before you've made it out of the driveway."

"Nonsense!" barked the man, as if his simple denial were proof enough that Newbury was lying. Veronica had met men like him before – those whose sheer faith in their own infallibility, their utter self-belief that they were *right*, led to an obstinate need to refute the word of others, even those who objectively knew better, lest they somehow emasculate themselves in the process of listening. To a man like that, conceding was tantamount to suicide. Which was, she reflected, exactly what he was about to do.

"Just for a moment," she said from where she stood by the window, "imagine that we're right, that there are machines out there in the grey, waiting to rend you limb-from-limb. Would you really wish to subject your wife to such horrors?"

The woman considered this for a moment, all colour draining from her face. "Ted?"

The man glared at Veronica. His cheeks flushed. "Madam, firstly, I place no credence whatsoever on your wild imaginings and fanciful stories, and secondly, if we were to encounter such a thing, I am quite capable of defending both myself and my wife."

Newbury shook his head in exasperation. "Sir, I really must…"

"You really must do *nothing!*" bellowed the man. All heads in the room turned to regard him – even the three waiters, who were otherwise leaning against the rear wall, with a general air of disinterest. "Nothing at all, you hear me! You will stay out of my way. I will hear no more talk of clockwork monsters." He jabbed his finger at Newbury's chest. "After all, they didn't kill *you*, did they?"

The woman swallowed. "Come along, Ted. Let's be off now, eh?"

Veronica stepped forward and caught her arm. "You don't have to do this, you know. You don't have to go with him."

The woman looked as if Veronica had slapped her. "He's my *husband*," she hissed, before turning her back on and leading him out of the door.

"Maurice," said Veronica. "We can't let them…"

"We don't have a choice. We tried. But they don't want to listen. All we can do is hope they see sense and turn back before it's too late. We can't detain people against their will, even for their own good."

Veronica chewed her lip. Why didn't these people *understand?*

The tension in the room was not dispelled by the couple's leaving. The other guests lapsed into an awkward near silence, as conversation muted and people glanced uncertainly at one another, as if waiting to hear another scream. Several moments passed. When no scream came, others began getting to their feet. A group of two men and two women – the ones who'd been sitting quietly by the fire – were walking in her direction.

"Look, if they can go, we can go too," said one of the women.

Veronica stared at her in disbelief. "I really don't think –"

There was a sudden, concussive bang at the window beside her. The sound made her start, and she spun on the spot to see, with horror, a man's hand pressed against the glass. As she watched, the splayed palm began to slide slowly down the slick surface, leaving a greasy smear.

"Is that –?" started the woman. Her voice had risen several octaves in pitch.

And then the white-haired man's face swam out of the greyness, thudding against the same pane, and one of the other men started screaming.

The face was slicked with blood, eyes wide in abject terror. It was held in the claw-like fist of one of the beak-faced automata. The man's tongue wagged as he tried to scream, but Veronica realised his jaw was hanging loose and broken, several of the teeth already scattered amongst the gravel. She couldn't tear her eyes from him as he was unceremoniously yanked back into the swirling fog, until all that was left was a bloody stain upon the window glass.

Somewhere in the distance, a woman gave a stark and guttural scream.

Veronica averted her eyes.

She felt Newbury's arm around her shoulders. "We did everything we could."

"Did we?"

"Yes, we did."

The four restless guests were silently returning to their seats by the fire, all thoughts of venturing out into mist long abandoned.

A short while later, Veronica – who had pulled the drapes over the windows to block out the view of the bloodied pane – watched as Newbury got to his feet and paced to the door. He was frowning.

"What is it?" she said, moving over to join him.

"Shhh!" He lifted his finger to his lips. After a moment, he turned to her. "Do you hear that?"

"What? No. Is someone coming? Sir Charles?"

"No. Music. Listen. There's someone singing."

Veronica took a step closer to the open door. She tilted her head. And then she caught it – a faint sound, drifting from somewhere else in the massive house. The strains of a woman singing, accompanied by the gentle tinkling of a piano. She stepped out into the hallway. It was louder here, like an echo, thrumming through the bones of the old manor. "What's going on in this place?"

"God knows," said Newbury, "but whatever it is, it's not normal." He glanced at his pocket watch. "How long has it been?"

"Since Sir Charles left? Nearly two hours."

"Too long," he muttered. He glanced across the hallway at the stairs. The threads of mist that had inveigled their way inside the house earlier had dissipated now, and aside from the eerie music and the utter lack of any other people beyond those in the dining room, everything might have appeared quite normal.

"They said they were going upstairs."

"You think we should go after them?"

"I think we've no other choice," she said.

Newbury gave a curt nod. He popped his head back around the door of the dining room. "We'll be back momentarily," he said. "I'll close this door behind me, and don't open it until you hear three knocks, like this." He rapped on the panel with his knuckle. One… two, three. Then again: One… two, three.

"Hold on! Where are you going?" called Miss Fotheringhay. She'd been subdued ever since Bainbridge had left, and Veronica didn't think it had anything to do with her earlier overtures to the terrified policeman. At least someone amongst the guests was taking the whole situation seriously. The poor woman was probably traumatised.

"Just going to find out what's taking them so long. Don't worry – we'll be back soon."

He pulled the door shut before she could object.

"Do you think it's wise to leave them?" said Veronica.

"No. But then, after what happened to the other two, I don't think they'll try anything stupid."

Veronica shuddered. It was too awful to contemplate. The man had been odious, but he hadn't deserved *that*.

"Besides," added Newbury, "there are three waiters in there with them if they need anything."

He crossed to the stairs and started up, the soles of his shoes scuffing against the polished marble.

At the top they paused on the square landing. Here, the floor was carpeted in plush red, and as the staircase swung around and continued to rise up behind them, presumably leading to the bedchambers and bathroom suite, the passageway narrowed, branching off in two directions. One towards the back of the house – along which Veronica could see a series of doors branching off into individual rooms – and the other along the side of the stairs, back towards the front of the house. No lamps had been lit up here, and it felt as if a caul of dingy gloom had settled over the place.

"Where do we even start?" she said, peering off into the shadowy passage. Newbury appeared to be considering. She ran her hand along the edge of the banister and felt something dry and gritty. She examined her fingers. Dust. The place was thick with it. "Doesn't look as though the servants are up to much," she said, presenting her hand to Newbury.

"No. It doesn't, does it?" He glanced up the stairs where they led to the second floor, disappearing into darkness, then indicated the narrow passage that led towards the front of the house. "Let's try along here. There must be other passages leading off deeper into the building."

Veronica wiped her hand on her dress and hurried after him, only to discover he'd stopped dead in the middle of the passage just a few feet ahead. He stooped down to examine something on the floor she couldn't see. "You've found something?"

Newbury stood, turning to reveal the object he'd retrieved from the carpeted floor: Bainbridge's cane. His face was ashen. He handed the cane to Veronica. She turned it over in her hands. It was unblemished, and the electrical instrument inside it had not been activated.

"It doesn't mean anything, Maurice. You can't assume..."

He swallowed, gave an almost imperceptible incline of his head, and then carried on down the passage to where it terminated in three separate doors – two on the right, and one directly ahead.

Veronica's mouth was dry. What *did* it mean? Had Bainbridge been caught unawares? Had he left the cane there for some reason? Had he meant for them to find it? Whatever the case, she didn't like it. And clearly, neither did Newbury.

Up ahead, he was opening doors and peering into the rooms beyond. She could still hear the eerie sound of the woman's singing, drifting faintly through the house like the final wisps of a dream upon waking, near forgotten. It was as if the music came from some other version of this creepy, unsettling house; as if it were an echo of a happier time, haunting the now deserted hallways and rooms. That was how it felt up here: empty and unloved. Even the air carried the damp, musty odour of abandonment.

"Veronica. Over here." Newbury's voice sounded tight, clipped. Raw. He was standing in a doorway, looking down at the floor beyond. His face was unreadable.

Please. Don't let it be. Not here. Not like this.

Slowly, she paced the remaining few steps to join him.

It was a body. There on the carpet.

Veronica flinched, barely able to look at it.

No. It can't be.

She took a deep breath to steady herself, then forced herself to look.

She felt a palpable flood of relief, followed by a sharp stab of guilt. It was Arun Singh, the man who had gone with Bainbridge to search for Fairfax. He was dead, lying in a pool of his own blood. His head was turned to the left, and the right side of his face was a gored mess.

His ear had gone. Taken.

"They've got him," said Newbury, through clenched teeth. "They've taken Charles."

THREE

"Do you think they're taking them as trophies?" Veronica was sitting at a small desk in the side room while Newbury examined the corpse. "The missing body parts, I mean."

"Perhaps," said Newbury. "It's difficult to tell. An arm, an ear… they seem oddly mismatched. In my limited experience, most trophy hunters are consistent. It's always the little finger of the left hand, or an eye; that sort of thing. An arm just seems… well, I don't know, really. Too *big* to be a trophy." He shrugged. "Until we get a better sense of what's unfolding in this house, we won't know for certain." He stood, stretching the muscles of his lower back. "One thing that *is* certain, though – those guard dogs out front aren't responsible for this. It's too targeted. Too precise."

"And Edwin Smythe?" asked Veronica.

"Same story. I think this is something different. Those automata – they lack the finesse."

"Finesse?" said Veronica, glancing at the bloody corpse. Not the word she would have used.

"You know what I mean. Outside, they tore those people apart and discarded them like animals. It was savage, uncoordinated." Veronica shuddered at the thought of poor Juliet, subjected to such horror. "But this – this happened for a reason. It's as if the killers have selected the body parts they wanted and taken them after the victim was dead. The bodies were even hidden from view after the fact. I'm convinced – there's two sets of killings going on here, by two different perpetrators."

Veronica shrugged. "Fairfax, then? He's the only factor we haven't accounted for yet."

"Maybe," agreed Newbury. "But there's more to it than that. I'm sure of it. Mr. Singh said Fairfax was his friend. He even intimated that they were close. Would Fairfax really have done this to his friend?"

"He might if he'd lost his mind. Or if they weren't such good friends as poor Mr. Singh seemed to think they were."

"Hmmm." Newbury stood with his hands on his hips for a moment, regarding the room, as if willing it to speak up and give voice to the things it had witnessed.

To Veronica, it appeared to be an office of sorts, the walls lined with several wooden bureaus and a dozen oak cubby holes, each of them stuffed with neatly rolled sheafs of paper. On the desk before her was a dusty felt writing slope. The ink in the wells had dried out and hadn't been replaced. "Fairfax can't have used this place much of late," she said. "This desk hasn't been disturbed for some time."

"Indeed. The marks on the carpet suggest the same. The dust has settled, and there's a crescent shape, here, where it's recently been disturbed by the opening of the door." He traced the mark in question with his finger.

"Which begs the question: what have the staff been doing?" said Veronica. "Why haven't they kept the place clean?"

"Quite. And why hasn't Fairfax made use of a room – or rather, what appears to be several *rooms* – that were once the centre of his operation?" He'd hastily checked behind the other nearby doors after finding the body, and they'd both been relieved to discover Bainbridge wasn't lying in a similar state behind any one of them. Just more disused offices, containing drawing boards, paper models and supply cupboards. "All these cubbyholes," Newbury went on, with a wave of his hand, "appear to contain blueprints for his various inventions. What happened to stop him coming here to consult them, or add to them?" Newbury rubbed thoughtfully at his chin. "Why hasn't he finished the drawing on the board next door? It's as if he just upped and disappeared."

"And once again, we come back to that same point made by Sir Charles," said Veronica. "If only we could find Fairfax, we'd be able to unlock the puzzle of this house."

The mention of Bainbridge seemed to stir Newbury, leading him to make a decision he'd been putting off. "Yes. You're right. We're not going to find anything more here." He took Bainbridge's cane from where it had been propped against the doorframe and held it out to her. "You know how to use this?"

"I've seen Sir Charles use it enough times," she replied, taking it from him. "I'm sure I can work it out. Why?"

"Because I want you to go back downstairs and keep an eye on the other guests. And I want you to be ready in case whoever is responsible for this shows their hand while I'm not there."

"Where are you going?"

"To find Charles."

She got to her feet. "Maurice, I don't think that's wise. We should go together."

"And leave those people down there to their own devices? You know what will happen. Someone else will decide to make a break for it and get chewed up on the driveway. Panic will set in.

They'll start wandering the house. And there's always the chance that the killer is going to show up, too, and they'll be defenceless." He shrugged. "You know I'm right."

She didn't want to admit it, but she did. "What happens if the same thing happens to you as happened to him? If you disappear and don't come back, what then?"

Newbury offered her a wan smile. "Then at least I'll be with Charles, and we can work it out together. You mustn't come after me, understand? If I'm not back within an hour, you hunker down in that dining room until dawn. When the fog has lifted, you can try to send for help, or make a break for it. You'll have more chance of getting the other guests to safety if you can see."

"I've told you before, you've got to stop trying to protect me all the time."

"Now you're just asking for miracles," said Newbury, laughing. "But it's not about you, Veronica. It's about saving as many lives as we can. Six people are already dead." His expression darkened. "Maybe more."

"You can't think like that. He'll be all right. You'll see."

"I hope you're right."

"Why is nothing in our lives ever *normal*? Wouldn't it be nice if, just once, we could go to a party without having to deal with people trying to kill us?"

Newbury touched her cheek with the edge of his thumb. "That's not the sort of life we chose."

Veronica sighed. "No. I don't suppose it is." She put her palm against his chest, pushing him lightly away. "Go on, then. Go and find Charles. You know where I'll be when you need me."

The look in his eyes spoke volumes. "Mind how you go."

Veronica swallowed, her mouth suddenly dry.

It seemed to him as if the house had swallowed him whole; as if this darkened passage were the long, quivering gullet of some leviathan beast, and with each slow, steady step he took along it he was willingly offering himself up as sacrifice, sustenance for whatever broken intelligence governed this strange, forbidding place.

Newbury knew that the notion was utterly ridiculous – that such thoughts were the mere whimsy of his mind, driven by fear and uncertainty and a deep-seated craving for a dose of the poppy with which he regularly diminished himself – but, nevertheless, he could not stop the thoughts from swimming unbidden out of his subconscious.

In the distance he could still hear the faint wailing of a woman's voice, the tinkling of the ivory keys of her piano. The music had taken on a sinister edge. He supposed it was the jolly timbre of the singing, the carefree sway of the rhythm, the insouciant conjuring of happier times. Juxtaposed against the bleakness of their situation, the deaths of the guests, the strange, sombre tone of the house itself, the music felt taunting, laced with dark intent.

More silly imaginings.

After he'd watched Veronica hurry back down to the staircase, Newbury had crossed the landing and set out to explore the rear of the house on this upper floor. Almost immediately, the atmosphere altered, and he'd become disorientated in the gloom. The passageways seemed longer than they should have been, the lighting dim and seeping in only through the sparse windows from the foggy world beyond. Portraits stared down at him from the walls, and what rooms he found continued the sense of abandonment he'd felt amongst the blueprints and drawing equipment. One room had been completely bare, the floorboards crumbling with damp, the wallpaper peeling from stained plaster. Another had housed a simple lavatory and basin, while a third was stacked with wooden crates, containing bundles of brass cogs, levers and wires.

The place didn't have the feel of a home. It wasn't *lived* in. Despite being recently built, it had the air of faded glory that he'd often sensed in country mansions owned by families that had fallen on hard times; that its glory days were long past, and the truth was now hidden behind a patina of pretence.

But if that were true, why still throw such lavish parties? And why not show your face? Newbury couldn't fathom Fairfax's motives. Did the man know that his automata were running wild in the grounds? Had he lured the guests there on purpose? If so, to what end?

Too many questions.

Newbury stumbled as he rounded a corner in the passage, catching his foot on a ruffled patch of carpet. He threw his hands up, catching hold of the dado rail to prevent himself from falling. After he'd righted himself, he stood for a moment, waiting for his eyes to adjust to the intense gloom.

Up ahead, on the left, a soft glow emanated from beneath a door. He hurried over. He could hear noises coming from inside; the gentle whirring of machines, the tell-tale *tick-tock* of clockwork.

"Fairfax? Is that you, man?"

He rapped on the door when there was no answer.

"Charles?"

A faint moan. A man.

Newbury turned the handle. The door swung open.

At first, he thought that a person had been strung up on the far wall; the flash of pink, emaciated flesh, the arms thrown out to either side, the limp head. But then, as he watched, the bearded figure lifted its head, fixing him with a sorrowful expression. Tears streamed down its cheeks. It opened its stark red mouth and emitted a slow, mechanical moan. A bright wound in its side oozed vibrant-coloured blood. A crown of thorns sat upon its head.

Jesus.

Fairfax had built a bizarre, mechanized chapel, here in the quiet depths of his house.

An entire chapel.

Newbury watched as the alarming, life-size figure – in truth another of Fairfax's automata – lowered its head again, lapsing into silence. Its outer shell was incredibly lifelike, modelled in painted plaster. Its chest heaved with unsteady breaths, as if close to death. The wounds in its wrists and ankles where it had been bound to a wooden cross were fashioned to look raw and ugly.

Newbury shivered. He'd never been a religious man, but something about this seemed deeply blasphemous and extreme.

A noise to his right startled him, and he turned on the spot, tensing – only to see that the walls had been covered in colourful enamelled murals, each of them depicting scenes from the life of Christ. What was more, these were the source of the clockwork sounds he had heard from outside. The images were animated, cycling through tiny, precise movements as they played out the scenes like mummers re-enacting a play. The wall on the other side of the room was the same, only the meticulously crafted images were all playing out different scenes.

The chapel must have taken him years to complete, a grotesque masterpiece.

Before the figure of Christ on the cross was a small rug and a copy of the Bible. This, then, was where Fairfax came to pray. A scientist with a deep and passionate faith. Perhaps not as contradictory as it might sound.

Was it a place raised out of devotion? Or penance? Whatever the case, it left Newbury feeling deeply uncomfortable. It seemed there was nothing simple about Fairfax and his unusual home.

As he watched, the figure of Jesus raised its head again, its glass eyes rolling back in their sockets as more blood began to bubble from its parted lips. It gave one, last, troubled exhalation, and was still.

Several people were arguing when Veronica returned to the dining room. She hadn't caught the full gist of the disagreement, but she gathered that one faction was proposing to put together a search party to go and look for her and Newbury, while another was vehemently opposed to the notion. They stopped abruptly as she closed the door behind her, turning the key in the lock. All faces turned towards her – all except the three waiters, who were still lounging against the back wall where she'd left them, faces a picture of studied disinterest.

See no evil, speak no evil…

"Where have you been?" said one of the men who'd been arguing. He was one of those who'd been making ready to leave a little earlier, just before the automaton had torn the other couple apart right before their eyes.

"Upstairs," she said, measuring her words carefully. "Looking for answers."

"And?" demanded Miss Fotheringhay.

"And Sir Maurice has remained to continue the search. We thought it best I return to keep an eye on things here."

"*You?* Keep an eye on –" started the woman, before stopping abruptly, her face creasing in a deep frown. "I say, isn't that Sir Charles's cane? I saw him carrying it earlier this evening."

Veronica sighed. "Yes, it is."

"So, you found him, then?"

"Has he located Fairfax?" cut in another man.

Veronica held up a hand for quiet. "I'm afraid Sir Charles is still unaccounted for. We found his cane in one of the passageways on the first floor. It's a big house, and he must have widened the scope of his search. Sir Maurice will endeavour to bring them all back shortly."

"But why would he leave his cane lying around like that?" insisted Miss Fotheringhay. "Surely he'd have taken it with him?"

"Yes, and what about Mr. Singh who went with him?" asked the first man.

Veronica decided there would be no benefit in telling them about Singh's body. Not yet. The tension in the room was already at fever pitch, a tinderbox waiting to go up in flames, and some more bad news might just be the spark that would ignite it. "Best not to speculate," she said, with a tight-lipped smile. "I'm sure we'll know more soon."

Miss Fotheringhay looked decidedly unconvinced. "But they will be all right, won't they? Both of them?"

Veronica squeezed Bainbridge's cane just a little tighter. "I'm sure they'll be fine," she said.

His left eye was gummed shut and there was a throbbing pain across the side of his head, radiating out from his left temple.

Bainbridge groaned and tried to shift his weight but couldn't seem to move his arms and legs. Close by, music echoed loudly; the shrill warbling of a woman baring her soul, and the *plinkity-plonk* of her piano. He'd heard it before, somewhere, but he couldn't place where.

He coughed, and tasted blood. It had dried on his lips; clotted in his moustache.

Slowly, he lifted his head, the muscles in his neck aching in protest. His right eye fluttered open. Everything was a blur, his vision swimming. A moment later, the left eye cracked open too, parting the lid of caked blood that had run down from the gash in his temple.

His first impression was of dank, grey stone, closing in from all directions. He fought a rising tide of panic; forced himself to steady his breathing. His chest wheezed.

He was sitting on a chair. No, he was *tied* to a chair, his arms pinned behind his back, his legs bound to those of the chair. He was alone.

Wincing, Bainbridge craned his neck, getting a measure of the place.

It was a cell, of sorts – more of a niche in a natural rock formation, a fissure or cleft in the bedrock. He was underground, that much was obvious. The ground was compacted earth, and above – although it made him feel dizzy and nauseous to look up – the fissure continued up into darkness. The scent of the place, from what he could tell beyond the iron tang of his own blood, was damp and earthy. The opening in the rock was a black rent, cast in shadow, wide enough to permit a single person at a time. The stone walls were bare. A lamp had been placed on the ground beside one of them, well out of reach.

Where was he?

He remembered going up the stairs with that fellow from dinner. Mr. Singh, that was it! He'd called out for Fairfax but received no reply. He'd gone off to explore one of the passageways, leaving Singh to check the rooms to the front of the house.

And then... nothing.

His assailant, whoever he may have been, had utterly blindsided him. Struck him with a blunt instrument of some sort, judging by the throbbing pain in his head and the fact he must have blacked out for some time.

Where was he now? Was this even still on Fairfax's property? *Under the house?* He supposed it was possible.

But why had they taken him? And why hadn't they killed him like that man he'd found in the library? His mind felt sluggish. He was missing something.

He searched the ground for his cane. There was no sign of it. Whoever had taken him prisoner, they'd been thorough. He tested his bonds, but the thin rope simply bit into his wrists, drawing more blood, more pain.

He spluttered again, hacking on blood that had trickled down the back of his throat.

It didn't look as though he was getting out of here any time soon. Besides, he was hardly in any shape to make a run for it, even if he were able to free himself.

Bainbridge closed his eyes and let his chin sink back down to his chest. The world was starting to swim. He just hoped Newbury or Veronica would get to him before it was too late.

**

The more he explored the house, the more Newbury's sense of creeping disquiet grew.

He'd left the unsettling chapel to delve deeper into the warren of linked passageways and rooms that comprised the rear of the property in this level. So far he hadn't met another living soul, nor a sign of anyone's recent passing. He felt overcome by a strange sense of dislocation, as if in wandering these rooms he had somehow left the real house far behind, to enter instead the murky domain of Fairfax's mind – a mind that – Newbury felt increasingly certain – was deeply troubled.

He struggled to make sense of what he was seeing. He'd found one room filled with dead and decaying pot plants – aspidistras left to go wild, now shrivelled to dead husks like the shed skin of so many huge arachnids. Another room was filled with strange works of art that, while lacking the precision and meticulous detail of the moving images he'd found in the chapel, nevertheless bore a certain untamed quality, despite the unusual subject matter – dead beetles at varying stages of decomposition, writ large upon the whitewashed walls in black gouache. Yet another room contained a taxidermised brown bear that had been wired to dance like an automated puppet as soon as the door was opened – faintly ridiculous, and at the same time vaguely terrifying, too.

There had been no sign of Bainbridge, and Newbury was growing anxious. He'd considered turning about and backtracking, perhaps going up a level to see if his friend had been taken to one of the bedrooms, but his every instinct told him that the answers to the puzzle of this house were to be found here, at the heart of this strange warren.

He followed the passageway as it made a dogleg, and then terminated in an open doorway. Candlelight flickered gently within, throwing out flickering shadows that behaved as if stirred by a breeze. Something metal glinted just inside the opening.

As he approached, he had the sense of a cavernous space beyond the door, at least the size of the ballroom on the floor below. He had no notion of where he stood in relation to his imagined floor plan of the building; the network of passageways had shifted direction so many times that he'd given up trying to keep track.

Slowly, he entered the room.

The first thing he noticed was the distinct chill. The room hadn't been heated for some time. Perhaps, he considered, he was now in some exposed wing or extension, branching off from the main house. It was impossible to tell – even if it weren't for the cloying fog, the windows here were barred with wooden shutters.

His footsteps echoed on the tiled floor as he walked.

It appeared to be Fairfax's main workshop, the place where the fellow assembled his inventions. Newbury had seen such places before – at the Chapman and Villiers factory, for a start – and recognised the higgledy-piggledy heaps of components, the stink of oil, the scattered cranks and spanners, pincers and eyeglasses. Here, a box full of fine-toothed cogs. There, a tray of mirrored eye lenses.

Two long rows of trestle tables had been set up, stretching the length of the room, running parallel from just inside the door to terminate a few feet from the far wall. Here was the only other door in the large space, opposite the one he'd entered by, this one closed.

He walked slowly along the centre aisle, as demarcated between the two rows of tables. The tables themselves were laden with all manner of partially constructed – or perhaps deconstructed – automata, from human-like limbs to hollow chest plates, from heads sprouting bundles of wires like hair, to strange goblin-like gnomes. Close by, one of them bore the almost complete shell of one of the creations he'd come to refer to as 'guard dogs', complete with its spindly-taloned hands and beakish face. Close up, it was like a design born from nightmare – the horrific approximation of a monster that could only have been imagined during the darkest of fugues.

Fairfax, it seemed to Newbury, had reinvented himself in the guise of some mad god, presiding over this ramshackle palace, manifesting his primal fears in the form of these terrible creations. Perhaps he really had set them loose on the grounds in the form of predators. Perhaps he took some insane pleasure from their wanton butchery.

Whatever the case, someone had been here recently – the lit candles, dotted around the edges of the room, were evidence enough of that.

"Who's there?" he said, wincing at the violence of his own voice in the otherwise silent space. "Fairfax? Are you here?"

The only reply was the echo of his voice, folded back at him. He took a step forward, intent on broaching the other door, but stopped when he glimpsed a shimmer of movement out of the corner of his left eye. He turned towards it, fists bunching by his sides in readiness.

"Hello?"

The creak of a wheel. The clatter of tin against tin.

Newbury watched, incredulous, as something stirred in the shadows. A figure – or rather, the upper half of a thing that resembled a woman – dragged itself forward into the light.

It was an automaton, of a sort – a half-complete mechanism that nevertheless had some semblance of life. The head and shoulders were extremely life-like. As with the figure of Jesus, the features had been modelled in plaster and painted to resemble flesh, although in this case several large cracks or missing chips somewhat tarnished the illusion. It had a torso, too, cladded in layers of tarnished tin plate, and two intact arms, each comprising an intricate array of brass rods, servos and cogs. That was where the resemblance to a human being stopped, as the machine's torso simply ended at the waist. Beneath that, a single wheel had been affixed to its flank, and it used this to drag itself along in a strange, lopsided gait, metal fingers scraping the floor with every movement.

To Newbury, it had the appearance of a project that had been abandoned halfway through construction, as if Fairfax had grown tired of it and had a better idea but had failed to put it out of its misery. There was something terribly melancholy about it. He wouldn't have been surprised to hear that it had affixed the wheel to itself of its own volition.

The thing regarded him with beady glass eyes, and its lower face attempted to form a smile, which looked more like a ghastly grimace, given that part of its top lip was missing. "Hello," it said. "I'm Angelene." Its voice was a chorus of fluting pipes. It shuffled closer, watching him expectantly.

"Newbury," he said. "I'm looking for your master, Fairfax. Have you seen him?"

The machine nodded enthusiastically. "I have seen him."

"When? Has he come this way?"

"Many times."

"Today? It's very important I find him."

Angelene made a face that he assumed was supposed to approximate sadness. "No. Not today. Not for eight-thousand-two-hundred-and-seventy-four hours. Is that a long time?"

Newbury's heart sank. "Yes," he said. "It's a long time." He indicated the door at the other end of the room. "What's through there?"

Angelene pushed suddenly at the floor, scraping herself back.

"What is it?" said Newbury. "What's the matter?"

"You don't want to go in there," said the machine woman. "Mr. Fairfax doesn't like it if you go in there. It's full of secrets."

Newbury glanced back at the door in a new light. "Oh," he said, with a crooked smile. "I like secrets."

"I think it's time you answered some questions," said Veronica, pulling a chair out from under the table and orienting it to face the three waiters, "don't you?" She sat down, folding her arms across her chest.

The three men barely seemed to react, continuing to study their gleaming boots.

"It's no use," said a man by the window, who had introduced himself earlier as Cordwainer Gray, a newspaper magnet from the American South. God only knew how he'd ended up here, trapped in a London mansion with the rest of them, but Veronica had neither the time nor inclination to ask. She shot him an enquiring look.

"I've tried already. When you were off with them others, looking for that policeman guy. They were just as tight-lipped then. Which sure leads me to thinking that the three of them done got something to hide."

Veronica had to admit she was impressed. It seemed someone, at least, had shown some initiative, rather than involving themselves in arguments or trying to concoct an outlandish plan to get away. She nodded gratefully, then turned back to the waiters. "Well?"

Still no response.

"Where is Mr. Fairfax?"

The man on the left gave a nervous twitch at the mention of his master's name, his whole body shuddering as if he'd been caught in a sudden cold breeze.

"You," said Veronica, singling him out. "What's your name?"

The man finally raised his head to look at her. His expression was as impassive as ever. He opened his mouth as if trying to form a reply, but no sound came out. After a moment, he returned his gaze to the floor.

"Just the same as they was before," said Gray, coming over to join her. "It's like old Fairfax has 'em so terrified they're afraid to speak up."

"Is that right?" said Veronica. "Is Fairfax responsible for what's going on here?"

The waiter on the right lifted his head suddenly and fixed her with a firm stare. "He is Two. I am Seven. The other is Four."

Veronica shook her head. "I don't understand. Seven? What do you mean?"

"I am Seven," the man repeated.

"They're talking absolute rot," said Miss Fotheringhay from somewhere behind Veronica.

"Playing stupid games," said another man. "When people's lives are at stake. It's not on."

Veronica waved them quiet. "Where is your master... umm... *Seven?*"

"It's like Mr. Valet already told you. He's indisposed."

"Mr. Valet?" Veronica sighed. "All right. But what exactly do you mean when you say 'indisposed'?"

"There's repairs need doing," said Seven.

"Repairs? To the house?"

The man's eyes looked shiftily from Veronica to Gray and back. "No more questions," he said, his voice level. "Questions will upset the master."

Veronica took a deep breath and let it out. "Well, I'm afraid that's not good enough, Mr. Seven, or whatever your real name is. People have *died* here tonight. So you're going to answer my questions whether you like it or not, and to Hell with what your master thinks."

Seven narrowed his eyes.

"You'll only upset the master if you open that door," said Angelene, scraping along the floor behind him. "You don't want to do that. He's not nice when he's upset."

Newbury knew he shouldn't feel sorry for this pathetic machine – it could hardly have *feelings*, after all, could it? – but something in its desperate tone tugged at his heartstrings. Whatever it was, this thing had suffered terrible abuse at the hands of its creator, and it seemed to comprehend that cruelty all too well, and to fear it, too.

He resolved to see what could be done to rescue the machine woman from such appalling conditions when this was all over. And any other of Fairfax's abandoned experiments, too. There was no doubt the man was a genius – to have created something with such self-awareness as Angelene was utterly profound – but his treatment of it was morally repugnant. To leave it alone up

here for nearly an entire year, suffering in isolation, incomplete…
If the man was prepared to gift his creations with such
intelligence, then he should equally be prepared to grant them the
equivalent dignity.

He reached the door.

"Please," said Angelene. "Please."

"I'm sorry," said Newbury. "I must. But I won't let him hurt
you for it. You have my word."

"What word?" said Angelene. "Do you need it back?"

Newbury smiled. He dropped into a crouch beside her and
peered into her strange, broken face. "No," he said. "The word is
freedom, and you can keep it."

Angelene frowned. "I don't understand."

"You will." Newbury stood and reached for the door.

"You won't like his secrets."

Newbury nodded. He turned the handle.

The first thing that struck Newbury was the clinical gleam of
the porcelain tiles, reflecting the bright electric light mounted on
the ceiling, its bulb bright and fizzing. The second was the dry air
and its mingling stench of bleach and carbolic, immediately
reminiscent of the countless trips he'd made to the police morgue
to examine victims' remains over the years. The third was the
desiccated corpse of a man laid out on a marble slab, naked and
devoid of its head.

He stepped into the room, turning on the spot, taking it all in.
Blueprints had been pasted up onto the walls, and surgical
apparatus rested in metal bowls and trolleys beside the slab. The
dead man's head sat on a workbench, skin now dry and taut,
teeth bared in a rictus grin. The eyes had been removed, but
something else, dark and glossy, resided in the sockets. The top
of the skull had been removed like a macabre cap and sat beside

it on the bench. It looked as if the head had been mummified, but Newbury wondered if it was the atmosphere of the room that caused the flesh to dry out like this, rather than putrefy; if it was never meant to have been left for so long.

Grimacing, he walked over and peered inside the skull cavity. It was filled with machinery, shining brass cogs and wheels, tiny switches and levers, like the workings of some huge, intricate watch. Everything was covered in a thin layer of dust.

Frowning, Newbury examined the blueprints. Pictured here were diagrams of the human nervous system, alongside detailed instructions for interfacing the spinal column into a mechanical brain stem at the base of the skull. He couldn't make sense of them all, but the gist was clear.

So *that's* what Fairfax had been doing here. Experimenting on people. Replacing human organs with his own clockwork devices. Hollowing people out from the inside and turning them into machines.

Newbury felt bile rising in his gullet.

"I warned you," said Angelene from the doorway. Newbury turned to look at her. She cocked her head to one side, echoing the gesture of the valet he'd met downstairs. "Secrets."

That gesture...

"Oh, God," said Newbury, realisation dawning. "It's the servants. They're all machines..."

And he'd left Veronica locked in a room with three of them. Not to mention a dozen civilians. He bolted from the room, his heart thudding.

"Don't leave me alone again!" cried Angelene, her piping voice receding into the distance as he ran. "Please..."

He lifted his head at the sound of footsteps, echoing off the cavern walls. They were coming his way.

Now that the bleeding seemed to have stopped he was beginning to regain his senses. His head still throbbed like the kick of determined mule, but the dizziness had abated somewhat. He'd tried to get more of a sense of his environment, but the only additional clue he'd been able to ascertain was the damp, earthy scent that seemed to hang in the air down here, reminiscent of a forest or woodland. He'd even fancied he'd heard a bird twittering, off somewhere in the distance, but had put it down to a flight of fancy, a symptom of his semi-delirious state. Unless, of course, they'd moved him somewhere onto the grounds of the house, and this fissure in the rock was amongst crags or outcroppings in an area of woodland.

He hoped that wasn't the case. If it was, there was little chance of him ever being found.

The footsteps stopped.

"Who's there? Show yourself." He eyed the jagged opening in the rock. "Come along! Fairfax, is it? It's about time you showed yourself."

A figure stepped forward into the weak lamp light.

"Ah, there you are…" Bainbridge trailed off as he realised who was standing there regarding him with that same cool, impassive expression he'd seen earlier: the valet, the elderly man who'd welcomed them when they first arrived. "You!"

The valet cocked his head to the side. "I'm sorry to keep you waiting, Sir Charles. I hope you're not too uncomfortable."

Bainbridge laughed, bitterly. "Well, I suppose you'd better untie me, then."

The other man didn't appear to share the joke. "I'm sorry. I'm afraid I can't do that."

"No. I didn't think so."

The valet took another step closer. Bainbridge could see now that he was carrying what looked disturbingly like a saw.

"What are you planning to do with *that?*"

The valet looked down at the saw as if seeing it for the first time. "You needn't worry, sir. It'll all be over soon, and you can go back to sleep. We just need to collect your donation for the master."

Bainbridge's mouth was suddenly dry. "What donation?"

For the first time since they'd arrived, the valet smiled. "Why, the soft part inside your head, of course."

"Well?" said Veronica. Her patience was wearing thin. "Are you going to answer me or not?"

The man who called himself Seven was still glowering at her, his stare unbroken, his jaw set tight. He looked as if he might snap at any moment.

She risked a glance at the others. Both were still staring at their feet.

Something wasn't right here. Men who called themselves by numbers, who refused to answer even the simplest of questions – even after people had been murdered in the very next room. They hadn't even reacted when the automata had torn apart that man on the other side of the windowpane.

Were they already traumatised? Too scared to speak? What the Hell was going on in this house?

She met Seven's gaze. She wasn't sure he'd even blinked. "Look, I just want to understand. Is Fairfax mistreating you in some way? Has he threatened you to stay silent?"

Seven's jaw was working back and forth. She could hear him grinding his teeth.

"Look, I think you should leave it for a bit," said Cordwainer Gray, who was now leaning against the table beside her. "He ain't looking too well."

"Are you all right?" Veronica said to Seven.

"Too many questions," replied the waiter, grinding the answer out between his teeth. "Too many questions."

"Look, why don't I fetch you a drink and –"

Seven lurched to his feet. His hand shot out, grabbing her tightly around the throat. He'd moved so quickly she'd had no chance to react. She tried to push him away, to take a step back, but his grip was like iron. The expression on his face was still disturbingly placid, but she could feel the ire radiating from him, a pure and passionate hate. "Too. Many. Questions," he screamed in her face. "Too many. Too. Many. Too. Many."

Beside her, Gray was bellowing something, and elsewhere a woman was screaming, but already they seemed so far away, as if they were in another room, another reality, a dream.

Veronica grabbed at Seven, trying desperately to prise his fingers loose, to ease the pressure on her throat enough to breathe, but it was no use. His thumb was digging into her flesh, compressing her airway, fingernails drawing beads of warm blood. She could feel her mind fogging, the darkness closing in.

"Too many questions. Too many. Too. Many. Questions."

FOUR

This was it. After everything, after all she'd been through, she was going to die here. At some godforsaken party, of all places, at the hands of an angry waiter. It was *ridiculous*. She would have laughed, if she'd been able to breathe.

Blackness limned her vision now. The world was fading. Or perhaps it was her that was fading, becoming slowly insubstantial, ghost-like, eroded. It made a strange kind of sense. The world was giving her up, letting her go, cut loose to drift away into nothingness.

She was vaguely aware that someone was trying to help her, grappling with the man called Seven, but it all seemed so far away now. Too much effort. Too many questions. Where had she heard that before?

The question irked her. Why couldn't she remember? *Why?*

There was a tremendous *crack*, and suddenly the pressure on her throat was gone. She sucked at the air, drawing it deep into her burning lungs. She wanted to scream at the agony of it all as the world came rushing back in from all directions.

She staggered back, clawing at her chest. Spots of light danced like baubles before her eyes.

"Miss Hobbes?"

It was Cordwainer Gray, his hand on her shoulder.

"Miss Hobbes? Are you okay?"

She nodded, still fighting to remember how to breathe.

She took in the scene. Miss Fotheringhay was standing over the body of the man named Seven, holding a chair and breathing heavily. One of the chair legs was broken. Seven's head was resting against the hearth.

Veronica shook her head, trying to process what she was seeing. The woman had knocked his head clean off at the neck. But that was... *impossible.*

Miss Fotheringhay dropped the chair. The body at her feet was twitching, yellow sparks spitting from the stump of its neck like tiny shooting stars, winking out on the carpet.

Veronica wondered for a moment if she was hallucinating.

"Miss Hobbes?"

She realised Gray had spoken.

"Wh... what... did you... say?" she asked, between bouts of fitful coughing.

"I said he was a goddamned automaton!"

Veronica, finally getting control of her breathing again, bent low to examine the twitching corpse. Sure enough, the remnants of a shattered mechanism were embedded in the fleshy stump, brass and cogs and oozing oil. He hadn't always been a machine, though; this was some sort of sickening hybrid, machine components installed in the body of a once-living man. A human being turned into an automaton.

Suddenly, the numbers made sense. *Two, Seven, Four...*

"So, I didn't kill him?" said Miss Fotheringhay. It was as much an assertion as a question. "It's just... I... I don't know my own strength."

Veronica lurched to her feet. Her head was still swimming, and she forced herself to focus, to hold the world steady through will alone. Behind the other woman the two remaining waiters – or whatever they were – had risen to their feet, suddenly alert.

"*Move!*" Veronica bellowed, and Miss Fotheringhay, startled, did as commanded, ducking to the left, just as Two's fingers closed on the space where her neck would have been. He glared at Veronica malevolently.

"The cane," she gasped, reaching her hand out behind her.

"What?" said Gray. "What are you talking about?"

"Sir Charles's cane! Hand it to me, *now!*"

The tone of her voice was enough to stir him to action. He scrambled to the table where she'd left the cane.

"Here, here! I've got it!" He placed it in her hand.

She hadn't taken her eyes off the other waiters as they cautiously advanced. She could only presume that, in seeing what had become of Seven, they were exercising more care, now that they'd lost the element of surprise.

She was still feeling slightly giddy from the oxygen deprivation, and she swayed slightly as she readied herself to fend off any further attacks.

The other guests were pressing themselves against the walls as if trying to make themselves disappear, or else hurrying for the exit. Veronica didn't suppose she could stop them now. She only hoped none of them would be foolish enough to rush outside.

The waiters were circling like predators, coming around in a pincer movement.

Still keeping the pair fixed in her gaze, she gripped the cane and twisted the metal knob at its head. It turned with smooth, machined efficiency. All along the shaft, slotted strips of wood began to unpack, lifting out on metal hinges to reveal a thin glass chamber within. Lightning sparked inside the glass, flickering white and blue as the centre of the cane began to spin, increasing steadily in speed, building to a charge.

"That's just... *wow*..." said Gray.

"Miss Hobbes, I'm with you," said Miss Fotheringhay, hefting another chair.

"And me," said a lean man in a green felt jacket, who'd dragged a poker from the pit of the fire and was wielding it before him like a sword.

She sent a grin in his direction. "Thank you."

"I'm Arthur. Arthur Emsworthy." He took a step back as the waiter known as Four lurched forward, grabbing for the poker and missing.

"There'll be time for introductions later," said Veronica, raising Bainbridge's cane. The metal tip was crackling with energy now, the glass chamber humming as the charge continued to build.

Almost... almost...

Two charged. Just like Seven, he was improbably fast, and he clearly intended to catch her off-guard. This time, though, she was ready for him, and she pivoted, bracing the head of the cane against her hip and swinging the tip up and round so that, as Two rushed in, his forward momentum caused him to impale himself on the electrified shaft. The tip tore a rent in his belly, plunging deep, even as the crackling electricity spilled out.

The waiter's body lit up, lightning crawling over his pale flesh as it blackened and burned. It danced between the teeth of his open jaws as the machinery inside his head began to sputter and fragment, sending sparks showering from his eyes like obscene tears. He jerked violently in a shambolic, dying dance. Veronica could feel the heat radiating off him; smell the rancid odour of roasting meat.

Moments later and the charge was spent. Two's body pitched backwards, still twitching, onto the carpeted floor. Smoke curled from his nostrils. His hair was singed and smouldering.

"Good God," muttered Cordwainer Gray. "I ain't never seen anything like it."

Veronica wrenched the cane free, turning towards the remaining waiter, Four, as he continued to advance on Emsworthy. It would be at least an hour before the weapon could be charged again, but it could still prove useful as a makeshift sword.

Four seemed to be weighing up the odds. He glanced from Emsworthy to Veronica, and then to Miss Fotheringhay. He seemed to make a decision – and pounced.

Emsworthy yelped and jumped back as Four lurched forward, and together they went down, hard, Four's mouth gnashing for Emsworthy's face as the man tried desperately to hold him off. The waiter had Emsworthy pinned to the ground. The poker had burned a hole right through Four's shoulder and now protruded rudely from its back, but it seems unperturbed by the injury, and more importantly, it hadn't slowed the thing at all.

"Miss Fotheringhay, if you would?" said Veronica, making way for the other woman, who was making ready to take another swing with her new chair.

"Bloody Hell!" screamed Emsworthy from the floor, pushing at the waiter's face, trying to keep his fingers from its snapping mouth. "Bloody Hell!"

"Ready?" said Miss Fotheringhay.

"Yes. Do it," said Veronica.

"*Stop!*"

The barked command caused Miss Fotheringhay to drop the chair, startled. Veronica looked round to see Newbury standing in the doorway, gasping for breath.

"Maurice?"

"Don't do it." He pushed his way through the press of fleeing guests. "We need one of them operational."

"We do?"

"Yes," he said, coming to stand beside her. He studied the still-gnashing automata as it straddled the prone Emsworthy on the carpet. "If we're going to find out where they're keeping Charles and get to the bottom of what Fairfax has been doing in this house."

"You're all mad," said Cordwainer Gray.

They stood in silence for a moment.

"Well, someone better get this bloody thing off me, then!" snapped Emsworthy.

The bodies of the two 'dead' waiters had been placed in the corner and wrapped in torn down curtains, and Gray and Emsworthy had rounded up all but one of the other guests, urging them to return to the dining room now that it had been secured.

Emsworthy had wanted to continue searching for the missing man, but Newbury had insisted that the guests all gather to hear the truth about what he'd discovered upstairs in Fairfax's workshop. With that news in mind, it didn't seem at all sensible for search parties to be wandering freely about the house. It was unclear how many other servants inhabited the property, and exactly what they might be programmed to do.

Now, everyone sat in stunned silence, many of them refilling their glasses to help combat the shock of what they'd been told.

There was no question of its veracity – the proof had been clear for all to see in the form of the dead waiters – but to hear the extent of Fairfax's madness was to truly comprehend the nature of their predicament. Had Fairfax invited them all there to be murdered?

Still, the only way to even begin answering that question was to find the man. A task that had so far proved beyond them.

Newbury had bound the remaining waiter, Four, to a chair by the fire. It – Veronica could no longer think of it as a man – had resumed its sullen expression and was refusing to meet Newbury's eye. The poker still jutted from its shoulder. It appeared to have no inclination to remove it.

"It's no use, you know," said Newbury. "We're going to find out anyway. We won't stop looking until we've torn this whole house apart and deactivated all of your colleagues." The waiter twitched at this, its right eye blinking involuntarily. "So, you might as well tell us what we want to know." Newbury leaned closer, until his face was nearly touching that of the automaton. "Where have they taken Sir Charles?"

The waiter finally lifted its head. The eyes swivelled to regard Newbury. Its jaw worked back and forth for a moment as it seemed to grapple with a response. For a moment Veronica expected it to lash out again, as it had several times already, straining against its bonds and trying to bite Newbury's face, but this time the fight seemed to have gone out of the thing.

Could an automaton feel dismay? Could it grow weary or anxious, or care enough about its counterparts to want to protect them? Whatever Fairfax had constructed here certainly had the capacity to mimic human interactions and emotions. Whether it could actually *feel* them – well, that was a question for the philosophers. It certainly showed no hint of fear, but surely the logic of the situation must have dawned on it, if it harboured even a glimmer of intelligence?

"In the down below. The world beneath," it said.

"Beneath where? This house?"

Four nodded reluctantly. "The master's realm."

"Fairfax is down there, too?"

Another nod.

"And what exactly is he doing?"

"Repairs," replied Four.

Veronica shivered. "Repairs?"

But Four seemed to have decided it had said enough, and its eyes dropped once more to the floor.

Newbury shifted in his seat to look at her. "There must be a way down. Somewhere inside the house. A passageway. A trapdoor…" He glanced back at Four. "Will you tell us the way?"

There was no reply.

Newbury got to his feet. "Then we'll find it ourselves."

Veronica grabbed his arm. "I don't like the sound of this. Repairs? Repairing *what*?"

Newbury sighed. "I have a horrible feeling he's talking about the staff."

"Then why take Sir Charl… oh," she said, trailing off as the full implication made itself abundantly clear.

The missing body parts.

Spares.

She squeezed Newbury's arm. "We'll find him."

He nodded. "Are you up to this? You know, after…"

"I'm fine," she said, aware of how ridiculous that sounded, given her croaking voice and the painful black bruises that had already flowered around her throat. "I'll be all right. I'm coming with you."

"Good." The hint of a smile. He turned to the room and its scared and weary occupants, who had started the night so bright and full of vivacity but were now looking haggard and forlorn. "Keep this one tied up and lock the door behind us. We're going to get to the bottom of this, once and for all."

Cordwainer Gray stepped forward, placing his glass on the table. "I'm going with you."

"I really do –" started Newbury, but he was cut off by another voice, a woman, speaking over the top of him.

"And me," said Miss Fotheringhay.

"I don't suppose I'd be able to live with myself if I didn't," said Emsworthy.

The three of them regarded Newbury and Veronica expectantly.

Newbury sighed, but it was a sigh of resignation, not defeat. "Very well…"

"In which case, we should all come," one of the others piped up. "Best we stick together."

"No!" said Veronica immediately. The last thing she and Newbury needed was to be distracted by a whole unruly gaggle of them. "We'll have to move quickly," she added by way of justification. "A small group is better."

"Miss Hobbes is quite right," said Newbury. "The rest of you, remain here. Please." They looked more relieved than disappointed.

Before he made for the door, Newbury crossed to Four and yanked the poker unceremoniously from the waiter's shoulder. "Might be needing that," he said, with a wink.

"This looks like the entrance to the cellar," said Emsworthy. He was standing beside a small wooden door set into the panelling beneath the stairs. It was open, and Veronica could feel a cool updraught swirling out from below. The persistent, eerie music seemed to be louder in there, too, echoing tinnily from the walls. She thought she was likely to have that woman's voice lodged in her dreams for weeks to come – provided, that was, that she made it out of there alive.

"That's got to be it," said Newbury, edging past Gray to take a look. He stood in the opening, peering down a narrow flight of stone steps. He'd taken a candle from the library, and the weak, flickering light seemed to paint pictures with the shadows.

They'd already tried exploring the kitchens at the very rear of the house, looking for a way down, but had found nothing but store cupboards and pantries filled with mouldering food, as well as the leftover remnants of the meal that had been served up earlier that evening. There were no staff about, thankfully, aside from an automated chopping machine mounted on a butcher's block, a headless contraption with three brass arms that reminded her of the violin player in the ballroom.

Similarly, the library had failed to reveal any secret passageways or trapdoors, as had the sitting room. Then Emsworthy had discovered this hidden door and they'd all gathered to take a look.

"Well?" said Veronica. "Do we risk it?"

"I don't see that we have a choice," replied Newbury, dipping his head as he stepped fully inside the small space. "Not with Charles still missing."

"Unless it's a trap," said Miss Fotheringhay.

"I'm sorry?"

"A trap. That *thing* could have been lying to us. Sending us down here to our doom." The last word was tinged with a hint of melodrama, although Veronica had to hand it to the woman – she had a point.

"This entire house is a trap," said Newbury. "We were lured here under false pretences. Our best hope of getting out lies in finding Fairfax and putting a stop to these damnable experiments he's been carrying out."

"I say we give it a try," said Gray, reaching for more gusto than he was able to deliver. He looked pale and scared, just like the rest of them.

"Me too," said Emsworthy, scratching nervously behind his ear.

Veronica looked to the other woman.

"Well, go on then," said Miss Fotheringhay. "Get moving before I change my mind."

They filed in behind Newbury, their every footstep ringing out on the damp stone steps.

"Unhand me now, you treacherous bastard!"

Bainbridge squirmed in his seat, fighting against his bonds, as the valet used a wax pencil to mark out a thin band across his forehead.

"Usually, we would shave one's head before making such an incision," said the valet, "but you have such lustrous hair, Sir Charles, that it seems only right to preserve it. You'll hardly see the mark after we've reattached the skullcap afterwards."

"I won't be seeing anything, will I? Because I'll be bloody well dead!"

The valet stepped back for a moment, regarding him with his odd, lifeless eyes. "Oh no. This is only a temporary measure, I assure you. Mr. Fairfax will soon set things to right. You'll be fully restored before you know it."

"Fully *restored...*" Bainbridge echoed, incredulous. "Do you even understand what you're doing here?"

"Yes, Sir Charles. We're carrying out necessary repairs."

Bainbridge knew then that there was no reasoning with the man. He was utterly insane. "Help!" he bellowed, trying once again to fight against the bonds that, even now, he could feel sawing into his flesh, drawing warm blood that ran down his wrists to gather in his palms. "Help me!"

"There's no one coming, Sir Charles. It's time to let us do our work." The valet took a white handkerchief from his jacket pocket and shoved it fiercely into Bainbridge's mouth. Then, signalling to two footmen waiting by the cave entrance, he grabbed Bainbridge by the collar and hauled him to his feet, chair and all.

The steps delivered them into a dank, empty cellar, that nevertheless felt crowded as the five of them crammed in, sharing the light of the lone candle.

The walls here were coated in a thick layer of green mould that gave off a wretched stench, and the floor was slippery and treacherous. Mouse droppings – and worse – were scattered hither-and-thither like foul seeds. A single wooden crate sat in one corner, so rotten now that it disintegrated as soon as Miss Fotheringhay touched it. The spilled contents revealed nothing of value – just the remains of an old dinner service, once carefully wrapped in newspaper and stored in straw, now as wretched as everything else in that miserable house.

What was of interest, however, was the narrow cleft in the facing wall, where the brickwork seemed to merge with the bedrock itself, presenting an opening that was about the width of a single person, and twice as tall. Veronica could see that carved steps continued down from the portal, roughly hewn into the natural rock.

Whatever lay beyond, it seemed to be the origin of the music. Veronica could make out some of the words now, as the woman sang a soft lament to lost love:

Once we lit up and danced,
And dreamed of romance,
But those lost, heady days,
Have all slipped away,
And the world has forgotten us, my love.
The world has forgotten our love.

Standing there, she had the sense of a massive, empty void, as if she were poised on the threshold of another world, as if to take a single step would be to transport herself to some imagined place, like Alice stepping through the looking glass. A realm conjured from Fairfax's twisted imaginings and ruled over by his grotesque creations.

"The down below," said Newbury, from beside her. "The master's domain."

She shuddered. "You think he's down there?"

"Fairfax, or Charles?"

"Either. Both." He examined the edge of the crevice by the light of the torch. "He must have found this place when he bulldozed the old manor. An underground cavern, right here in the bedrock beneath the city. He built his new house right on top of it."

"But why?"

"Because the man should be in an asylum," said Emsworthy, from behind them. "There's no fathoming a mind like that."

"No," said Newbury. "I don't suppose there is. That's been the problem all al –" He was cut-off by the sound of someone shouting down below, down in the deep darkness of the cavern.

"Help! Help me!"

"Charles!"

Newbury took off, launching himself down the uneven steps and taking their only source of light along with him. Veronica plunged after him, the others bringing up the rear.

"Charles! We're here. We're coming!" Newbury shouted, his anxious voice ringing out, cutting across the sound of the music.

As they descended, Veronica realised the flight of steps was slowly curving to the right, following the natural sweep of the cavern wall. The narrow passage was beginning to open up, too, and for a moment she had the disturbing sense that she was plunging into nothingness, an ocean of gloom and shadow into which she might tumble and drown. But then light seemed to burst out of that endless night, and suddenly the entire scene unfolded before her.

The steps continued down for another fifty feet or so, hugging the ragged wall on one side, but open to the cavern on the other. The space was huge – about a hundred foot in each direction – and peppered by enormous stalagmites. Most bizarrely, the walls were covered in an abundant fungus, the enormous caps of which gave off a warm, gentle glow. And there were trees. A small woodland's worth of trees, growing out of the packed earth between the jagged stalagmites. Oak, ash, pines.

How was that even possible, with no apparent source of sunlight? The whole place was filled with the scent of their rich sap. Had the trees been transplanted and brought down here... or had they grown from saplings in this subterranean world?

And it really was an unground world, a tiny kingdom of the down below.

"Here they come!" barked Newbury, jolting Veronica from her musings..

She turned to see three footmen – or rather, automata dressed as footmen – come charging up the steps towards them.

Ahead of her, Newbury braced himself against the wall, readying the poker. She did the same, clutching Bainbridge's cane in both hands. Behind her, the two men were rolling up their sleeves, and Miss Fotheringhay had produced a carving knife from under her jacket, presumably appropriated from the chopping machine they'd found in the kitchens.

The first of the footmen reached Newbury, hands grasping for his jacket. Newbury twisted, catching the automaton under the jaw with his elbow and then slamming it back against the cavern wall. Its head bashed against the rock with a resounding crack, and it lolled for a moment, before seeming to bring itself around, thrashing out at Newbury, grabbing hold of his arm. Calmly, Newbury leaned closer, buying himself leverage, and forced the poker up beneath the automaton's chin. With a sudden upward thrust, he punched the iron rod through the skull and sent the machine man tumbling over the side of the steps.

Meanwhile, the other two footmen had scrambled past the battling Newbury to get at Veronica and the others. Emsworthy and Cordwainer Gray were grappling with one – Emsworthy pinning it while Gray battered at it with his fists –and Veronica traded blows with the other, knocking it back with Bainbridge's cane every time it tried to close the distance between them.

The sight of its dead eyes and grasping hands caused her stomach to flip, reminding her of what had happened back in the dining room, and she gritted her teeth and pushed through the fear and anxiety, roaring as she forced her way forward, battering the automaton back, step-by-gradual-step, until at last, with a final, incoherent wail, she raised her foot and planted it against the thing's thigh, shoving it backwards off the steps.

It made no sound as it fell, not until it crashed upon the uneven ground below, fragmenting like a porcelain doll dropped upon a tiled floor.

All the while, the music played on, incongruous against the appalling violence.

Behind her, Miss Fotheringhay had stepped in to help finish off the last of the footmen, sawing at its bloodless neck with the carving knife while the two men held it down. Her expression was set in a fierce grimace. As Veronica watched, the head popped loose, spilling a slew of clockwork components into the steps.

They left the thing where it had fallen and carried on down the steps at a run.

"Charles? Can you hear me? Charles?" Newbury took the last five steps at a jump, rounding a tall stalagmite and disappearing from view.

Veronica hurried after him.

Down here it was like walking through some prehistoric remnant, a wild place forgotten by time. Ferns brushed her shins, and emerald moss carpeted a vast expanse of the rocky ground. Tree roots wormed through the moist loam and giant leaves flapped listlessly in a cool breeze. Somehow, sunlight must penetrate the stone canopy above, she realised, falling in bright shafts on the lush greenery below. Now, though, the only light came from the knots of strange, luminous fungus that clung to the walls and ceiling.

Somewhere above her a bird cawed, as if in warning.

"Maurice?" she called, unsure which route he had taken through the pathless undergrowth.

"Follow the music," came his shouted reply.

He was right – down here the music was noticeably louder and seemed to be emanating from somewhere in the bizarre woodland.

Feeling slightly disoriented, she stumbled on, trying to home in on the sound. Behind her, Emsworthy led the others in pursuit.

She caught up with Newbury a few moments later, on the edge of what appeared to be a small clearing at the heart of the cavern. Here, the trees had been cleared, or otherwise formed a natural, open theatre.

Theatre was the right word for it, too, for the scene had apparently been dressed like a stage. A man sat in a wing-backed armchair with his back to them, only the top of his head and the elbow of his left arm visible from this angle. Beside him, a gramophone sat on a wooden stand, the needle juddering in the groove as the wax disc – the recording that had been echoing so persistently through the house above – revolved on the turntable. A small mahogany desk had been set up at the far end of the clearing, along with a drinks cabinet and an array of neatly arranged glasses and decanters. There was even a small, well-appointed bookcase, although the spines of many of the books had slumped, encouraged towards dissolution by the damp. The moss formed a deep, soft carpet underfoot.

Newbury stood amongst the boughs of two trees, looking on in evident amazement. "Could you ever have imagined?" he said, his voice almost reverential. "A place like this, down here, beneath the smog and the grime. An oasis, hidden away by the city."

"And the home of a killer," said Veronica.

Newbury nodded. He glanced across at her, and then together they strode out into the clearing.

"Fairfax?" said Newbury, raising his voice to be heard over the music as they walked up behind the seated man. "It's over."

The man in the chair didn't move.

Veronica crossed to the gramophone and yanked the needle out of the groove. The woman's warbling voice cut off abruptly. The ensuing silence seemed stark by comparison.

"Fairfax! I know it has to be you. Will you cease these ridiculous games and answer me!" Newbury, aggravated, circled around the front of the chair. "Fairfax...?" His voice trailed off. He stood for a moment, staring at the man in the chair.

Confused, Veronica circled round to join him. She was vaguely aware of their three companions emerging from the tree line, bringing up the rear.

At first she thought the man in the chair was sleeping, his head rocked forward so that his chin rested upon his chest, his arms folded neatly upon his lap. He was dressed in a smart black suit, but it looked somewhat faded now, with odd stains around the shoulders.

Then she realised what was wrong. One of the man's ears was puckered and bloody and, despite the pale pink hue of the rest of his face, was alarmingly brown. It had been roughly sewn into place. She took a step closer, her hand going involuntarily to her mouth to stifle a scream, as she saw the same was true of his arms – the one on the right was bulkier and longer than the other, the hands horribly mismatched in size and colour. The closer she came, the more she understood that the figure she had at first assumed to be Fairfax was, in fact, a grotesque patchwork of human body parts, stitched together to form a ghastly whole; an effigy of flesh and bone, cast in the shape of a man. Blood and other fluids had seeped through the front of his white shirt, and ropey lines of black stitches were visible around the base of his neck where his shirt collar had fallen open.

"Good God," muttered Newbury. He crossed to the figure, gingerly checking for a pulse at its neck. He glanced at Veronica and gave a little shake of his head. "Another of Fairfax's experiments?"

Veronica didn't know how to respond. Was this why they'd taken Bainbridge? To be butchered so his components could form a part of this appalling golem?

"How dare you disturb the master's sleep?"

The familiar, monotone voice had come from the edge of the clearing behind them. Newbury and Veronica turned as one to see the valet, flanked by two footmen, standing beneath the shadows of a huge oak tree. Bainbridge was on the ground before them, bound to a chair that had been pitched on its side, so that his face was buried in the thick moss. He'd been gagged, and someone had drawn markings across his forehead. His eyes were wide and panicked, pleading. The valet was holding a saw.

"Your master?" said Veronica. "You mean that *thing* is Fairfax?" She waved her hand in the direction of the patchwork corpse.

"Who else?" replied the valet, cocking his head.

"But... look what you've done to him," said Newbury. "He's been dead a long while."

The valet and the two footmen all shook their heads in sync.

"No," said the valet, "he's just sleeping."

"You're wrong," said Newbury. His voice was tinged with sadness. "All those people. Why? Why have you done this?"

"He malfunctioned," said the valet. "He stopped working. So we did what he has always done for us. We fixed him. We found the spare parts required, and we replaced his faulty components."

"And still he hasn't woken up," said Veronica. "So you keep going." It was so desperately sad. The most heinous crimes had been committed here, but in a way, these machines – and not least the men they had once been – were as much the victims as the people they had killed.

"The master must be repaired," said the valet. "We must find what is broken and make it new."

"No," said Newbury. "You must stop. *Now*. Your master cannot be repaired. He's gone."

"He is sleeping," repeated the valet. "We have brought him to his favourite place and surrounded him with his favourite things. When he wakes, he will be happy again." He brandished the saw. "The soft material inside Sir Charles's head will see to that."

On the ground, Bainbridge squirmed, and Veronica fought the urge to rush to his side. Instead, she slowly shifted his cane behind her back and gave the metal head a sharp twist. She felt the shaft begin to unpack as before.

Newbury took a step towards the group of automata. "Let him go. Even if you were to take Sir Charles' brain, it wouldn't make any difference. There's nothing left of your master now.

You've replaced so much of him that he barely even resembles the man who created you."

The valet's lips twisted into an animalistic snarl. "You know nothing of the master. His will is absolute. He *will* conquer this. He *will* wake again."

Newbury sighed. "I suppose we'd better get this over with, then." He shifted his stance, bringing his fists up defensively.

The valet charged, swinging the saw like an axe in both fists.

Without thinking, Veronica sprung forward, swinging the transformed cane around before her and meeting the oncoming valet, battering the saw out of Newbury's way and plunging the tip of the cane deep into the valet's chest.

She released her grip on the handle, shoving his spasming body away from her. As before, the electrical discharge flooded his chest, crawling over his flesh, causing pockets of tiny mechanical devices to detonate, erupting like sparking volcanoes from the valet's dead flesh.

He stuttered and fell to the ground, his body a smoking ruin.

Newbury looked at her with something approaching awe.

On the edge of the clearing, Emsworthy, Gray and Miss Fotheringhay had moved in on the two remaining footmen and wrestled them to the ground, deactivating them with the carving knife. It wasn't the most elegant approach, but it certainly sufficed.

Newbury ran to Bainbridge's side, using the valet's discarded saw to hastily cut through his bonds. Once free, Bainbridge yanked the handkerchief from his mouth, spitting and screwing his face up in disgust.

"About time!" he said, as Newbury helped him up to his feet. "They were about to get busy with that saw. What kept you?"

Newbury grinned. "I'm pleased to see you, too, Charles."

Bainbridge shook his head. He looked to Veronica. "I'll tell you what else," he said, holding out his arm so she could see.

"What? Are you hurt?"

"No." He shot her a broad grin. "That bloody cufflink has come undone again."

It rained for Juliet's funeral.

Apt, really, for such a melancholy affair. Veronica was pleased that the turnout had been so considerable, despite the inclement weather. She'd stood by the graveside holding Newbury's hand as the rain drummed on the coffin lid and the vicar droned on, and then it was over, and she was standing inside the chapel, soaked through to the skin, left to her memories of the woman who had taught her so much that she still held dear.

It had been nearly two weeks since the events at Fairfax's house and the men of the Yard, directed by Bainbridge, had carried out a deep and thorough search of the premises. More bodies had been discovered, and it seemed that Fairfax, along with his creations, were to be held responsible for at least twenty murders, including those of the staff themselves, whose bodies had been co-opted for his experiments. Now deactivated, their remains were to be returned to their families for proper burials.

It transpired that Edwin Smythe was one of several victims from a party held the previous evening – the automata had taken to holding such dinner parties in the name of their host, in order to lure a fresh supply of spare parts to the house for their macabre repair work. Too many people had lost their lives, but at least that would be the end of it now.

The 'guard dogs', as Newbury had named them, had also been decommissioned and impounded by the police. They'd returned to their nest beneath the house with the coming of the dawn, and as the fog slowly lifted, the guests – and their drivers, who'd been holed up, none-the-wiser, in a separate outbuilding drinking and playing cards – made good their escape. Within hours the place had been crawling with police, and the guests were all being checked over at the hospital. The injuries of the survivors were minor, but Veronica didn't doubt that the effects of that terrible evening would be felt by them all for a long while after.

She looked up. On the other side of the chapel, Bainbridge was deep in conversation with Miss Fotheringhay – Cynthia, as she'd since insisted. He looked happy. A few others from the party were there too – Emsworthy among them – but she'd heard Cordwainer Gray had already set out for America. She couldn't say she blamed him.

She felt Newbury nudge her shoulder and turned to loop her arm through his.

"You know, you saved me again, back there, when that valet was coming for me with the saw."

Veronica grinned. "I know. We keep doing that, don't we? Saving one another."

"I think it's becoming a habit."

"Well, it's certainly not one *I'm* going to discourage." She tugged on his arm. "Come on, let's get out of here."

"All right," he said. "But what about Charles?"

"Oh, leave him," she said, leading him out into the rain. "It's about time he found a bit of happiness, even if it is only fleeting."

Newbury smirked. "The old dog. I just hope she knows how to operate cufflinks, otherwise the whole thing's doomed…"

ABOUT THE AUTHOR:

George Mann is a *Sunday Times* bestselling novelist and scriptwriter. He's the creator of the *Wychwood* supernatural mystery series as well as the popular *Newbury & Hobbes* and *Tales of The Ghost* series, two of which are in development as television shows. He's written comics, novels and audio dramas for properties such as *Star Wars*, *Doctor Who*, Sherlock Holmes, *Judge Dredd* and *Dark Souls*. He is currently part of the writer's room on several forthcoming genre television shows.

George lives near Grantham, UK, with his wife, children and two noisy dogs. He loves mythology and folklore, Kate Bush and chocolate. He is constantly surrounded by tottering piles of comics and books.

Also from NewCon Press

Steampunk International edited by Ian Whates

English language edition of an anthology showcasing the very best Steampunk stories from three different countries: UK, Finland, and Italy; released by three different publishers in three different languages. UK contributors are George Mann (an original Newbury and Hobbes tale), Jonathan Green, Derry O'Dowd.

Best of British SF 2021 edited by Donna Scott

Two dozen of the best stories written by British and British-based authors during 2021, as selected by series editor Donna Scott. Features stories by Paul Cornell, Liz Williams, Keith Brooke and Eric Brown, Aliya Whiteley, Fiona Moore, Nick Wood, Martin Sketchley, and more.

The Double-Edged Sword – Ian Whates

Fleeing a backwater town one step ahead of the law and tiring of his dubious life style, the Fallen Hero seeks employment in the port of Cray. But his past catches up with him and he is forced to embark on what looks to be a suicide mission… unless he can beat the odds.

Embertide – Liz Williams

Practical Magic meets the *Witches of Eastwick*. Life has resumed a semblance of normality for the Fallow sisters, but that's never going to last. It's not long before they face dangers beyond their understanding; threats that straddle the contemporary world and the mystical.

On the Brink – RB Kelly

Danae Grant is trying to build a new life as a post-etheric citizen, determined that nobody will ever touch her again. In Danae, Adam sees a potential entry point into the city's secretive a-naut community. In Adam, Danae sees the threat that could end her very existence.

www.newconpress.co.uk